S0-BBW-537

SAINT CATHERINE LABOURÉ
AND THE MIRACULOUS MEDAL

SAINT CATHERINE LABOURÉ
AND
THE MIRACULOUS MEDAL

Written by Alma Power-Waters

Illustrated by James Fox

IGNATIUS PRESS   SAN FRANCISCO

© 1962 by Alma Power-Waters
Copyright renewed: © 1990 by Brian Power-Waters
All rights reserved

Originally published by Farrar, Straus & Cudahy, Inc.
A Vision Book

Published by arrangement with Farrar, Straus and Giroux, LLC

Cover art by Christopher J. Pelicano
Cover design by Riz Boncan Marsella

Published by Ignatius Press, San Francisco, 2000
ISBN 978–0–89870–765–6
Library of Congress catalogue number 99–75402
Printed in the United States of America ∞

Manufactured by Thomson-Shore, Dexter, MI (USA); RMA83JM00, September, 2015

CONTENTS

I

OFF TO SENAILLY

WHEN PIERRE LABOURÉ was about to take his six youngest children on the annual trip to the French village of Senailly, he would gravely ask:

"Who wants to sit on the driver's seat with me?"

Naturally, all six wanted to. It was the place of honor. What Pierre really meant was, who wants to start out on the driver's seat, for each one eventually had his turn. He asked the question to see the excitement on the children's faces.

It was a warm June morning in the year 1815, and the village in which the Labourés lived was on a green shelf of land high up in the Côte d'Or in the province of Burgundy. The village was called Fain-les-Moutiers.

The air was filled with midsummer, the sky cloudless. Outside in the lane a shepherd passed silently, on his way to the valley with his flock. But inside, the house was filled with expectancy.

Mama Labouré bustled around the kitchen, putting last-minute things into the goat-hair trunk. The children raced here and there, remembering something they "simply must" take with them to the house that had been Grandmère's. Here it was that they spent their summers.

"Well," asked Papa again, "who is it going to be?"

"Oh, let me sit in front! Let me, Papa!" cried Tonine, who was nearly seven and well able to make her voice heard over the din the boys were making.

"It's my turn!" piped little Auguste, the baby of the family, repeating what his brother Pierre said. Charles, at fifteen, considered himself too grown up to ask for a turn on the driver's seat, though he was just as eager as the others.

Twelve-year-old Joseph was polishing the shoes that Mama was waiting to pack. Then they would be ready to wear for Sunday Mass at Senailly. During the week the children wore sabots, wooden work shoes.

A month before, in May, Zoé had had her ninth birthday. She was dark-haired, with large dark eyes and sturdy legs, a shy, serious child and her father's favorite. While the others vied for the seat of honor, she stood silently looking out of the window, watching the horses being harnessed.

Zoé was a pet name, given her because she happened to be born on May 2, 1806, the feast day of Saint Zoé. Her baptismal name was Catherine.

The children pulled at their father's coat sleeve or grabbed him around the knees. He was a tall man and good looking, lean and strong from years of plowing.

"Children! *Tais-toi!*" Mama came into the parlor with her hands clapped over her ears. "Have done! You're making more noise than two trees full of magpies."

"We'll soon settle this question." Papa's eyes fell on Zoé, who was still intent upon the horses. "Zoé shall sit with me because she didn't ask to."

There was no more to be said. Even the smallest in the Labouré family knew that when Papa made a decision he never changed his mind. He was a loving father but a strict one. None dared to contradict him. Pierre was deeply religious and firm; Madeleine, his wife, soft, gentle, and saintly.

Tonine hid her face in her pinafore and began to sob. Papa had no patience with tears. "Antoinette!" he warned, frowning at her. "Stop at once."

The child was so astonished at being called by her baptismal name that she only cried harder.

Papa hurried to the kitchen. "I must get the trunk shut or no one will go anywhere."

"Never mind, Tonine", Zoé said, tying the bow of the sunbonnet under her little sister's chin. "I would much rather you sat in front. But you know we must do as Papa says." Then, with her usual gentleness, she added, "You can take charge of Ninette and her kittens."

Tonine's face brightened. "Where are they?" she asked, wiping away the tears with the back of her hand.

"In the shoe box. And Ninette is in her basket." Tonine scampered off.

Joseph took care of Auguste, who had already forgotten about sitting in front. "I'll give you some of my tadpoles and froggies if you're a good boy", he promised, leading the small boy by the hand out to the wagon. "You watch me put my boxes of books and my fishing tackle in. Then you can have the froggies."

Nine o'clock was ringing from the church steeples in the valley as the Labourés were ready to leave. The newly-painted red wheels of the wagon flashed in the sunlight. One of the farmhands had woven a bright ribbon into each of the horse's plaited tails.

"Look, children, at the ribbons. Aren't they festive?" cried Mama happily. "Come, Zoé. Come, Charles, Joseph, Pierre. Where's Tonine? Oh, there you are! I have the lunch basket. Here Auguste, *bébé*. Mama is waiting."

Just as everyone had climbed aboard and Papa had his hands on the reins, the rosy-cheeked maidservant came running out of the kitchen door with a huge stone jar of lemonade in her arms.

"Oh, thank you, Marie", said Mama gratefully. "I brought the wine and forgot the lemonade. And on such a hot day, too."

Zoé and Tonine wore sunbonnets and pinafores over their dresses, and the boys in their long cotton pants had wide-brimmed straw hats perched at jaunty angles on their heads. The Burgundy sun was hot.

At the back of the wagon was a bed of fresh hay in case Auguste wanted a nap. Charles, Pierre, and Joseph had brought books to read. Ninette protested loudly in her closed basket, while Tonine cradled a rag doll in her lap, as well as the precious shoe box. She sang a lullaby softly as the wagon wheels squeaked along the dry rutted road.

Sitting up in front, Zoé clung close to her mother. Neither of them wore sunbonnets now. Papa had insisted upon having the top of the wagon up over the seat. Zoé knew Mama liked to see the sky overhead, but she also knew that her mother would never protest against anything Papa wanted.

"Your father is much wiser than I", she always said in answer to childish whys. She had a gentle way of drying tears in a few minutes.

Her name had been Madeleine Gontard when Pierre Labouré first met her. Well educated, quietly charming, she taught school to earn a living. Pierre himself had at one time studied for the priesthood. He knew a great deal of history and Latin and had read many learned books. Feeling that he was not suited to the religious life, however, he had turned to farming. Now, after twenty years of working from dawn to sunset, he was the most successful farmer for miles around. The people of Fain-les-Moutiers admired Pierre and his family so much that they had chosen him to be their mayor.

Zoé liked to see her father wearing his linen smocks over his trousers when he worked in the fields, because Mama had made them and smocked them, too. Sabots protected his feet from the soggy wet fields.

Perhaps she was most proud of Papa when he took the whole family to Mass on Sunday. He looked like a schoolmaster, some said, with his frilled shirt, his black cravat, and high-crowned hat. His bearing was soldierly.

They were driving now on a narrow road that ran beside a wood. The heat was unbearable. A woman standing at the door of her cottage waved to them with friendly Burgundian courtesy.

"I'm thirsty", young Pierre announced.

"We could all do with a refreshing drink", Papa agreed, mopping his brow with a cambric handkerchief. "What do you say, Madeleine?"

She turned her head back over her shoulder and asked the children to help her. "We'll stop now and have something to eat. We've been on the road a long time."

Papa consulted his watch. "Nearly two hours. We must water the horses."

Soon they were sitting under a great tree in the wood, the picnic things spread out. "Oh, Mama, plum pie!" cried Joseph, round-eyed.

Although Madeleine had filled a large basket, such as vinegrowers use, with slices of cold meat and bread, in no time everything had disappeared.

Auguste, clutching a half-eaten butter bun in one hand, darted about like a grasshopper, his cheeks as red as field clover. Eating a juicy pear, Joseph sat propped against a tree trunk, a book open on his knees.

"What are you reading, Son?" Papa asked.

"A book on chemistry, Papa. It's one Antoine left behind when he went to Paris."

"Good, good", said his father, stretching himself on the grass with a groan of pleasure. "Better to read a book than let it get musty.

You know, Madeleine," he paused a moment, "I can hardly believe Antoine is eighteen years old. And Hubert, twenty-one! Now that they're in Paris, we will be lucky if we ever see our sons again."

"Ah, now, Pierre," said Mama, "they are good boys and write often. It is more than many children do."

"Will Marie-Louise come to see us this summer?" Zoé asked, leaning her head against her mother's shoulder.

"Hard to say, *chérie*. Since your oldest sister went to live with Aunt and Uncle at Langres, she goes wherever they go."

Papa sat up suddenly and looked at his watch. "Oh,

come, come, we'll have to get on our way. I must get back to Fain this afternoon, after I see you settled at Senailly."

"Hurry then, children, all of you", Mama said. "Help me put the things together. Here, Joseph . . . the basket."

Young Pierre, thirsting for adventure, protested. "Can't we stay a bit longer? It's so nice and cool."

Papa got to his feet. He gave a hand to Mama and pulled her up gently. "Sorry, Son," he said, "but the farm won't run itself."

"It's Pierre's turn to ride in front, isn't it?" asked Zoé, to ease her brother's disappointment.

On picnics Mama carried a small bag containing a piece of folded flannel and a sliver of soap. "There's a brook under the tree over there", she said, handing Zoé the bag. "Dip the flannel in the water and wash Tonine's face and hands, and Auguste's too."

As the three children ran to the brook, Tonine fell over a sharp stone and cut her knee. She bore the pain bravely for a few minutes, but on their return she began to cry. Zoé knelt down and with the clean, wet flannel wiped away the specks of dirt surrounding the cut.

"Oh! That hurts", wailed Tonine, her face puckered up.

Zoé put her arm around her sister's shoulder. "Stay there while I dip the rag in the brook. Then I'll bind up the cut. The cold water will take away the pain."

Small Auguste looked on with great interest, a

chubby finger in his mouth. Zoé, never happier than when she was helping someone, took Tonine's arm as she hobbled along.

Auguste ran ahead with the news. "Tonine fell! Tonine fell over a big stone!"

Mama was not in the least disturbed. "If Zoé's taken care of the cut, everything is all right", she said with perfect confidence. "Hurry, now, don't keep Papa waiting."

Pierre sat in front with his father. Mama got into the back, hoping to persuade Auguste to take a nap. He was only five years old and had been running around since daybreak.

"Climb on my lap", she coaxed, as the other children scrambled back into their places. She held out her arms. But Auguste had enough childish wisdom to know that if he went to sleep he might miss something.

"Must have had a great downpour here", Papa observed. "The road is full of deep ruts." He slowed the horses.

A farmer mounted on a fat donkey was coming toward them. He smiled broadly and doffed his battered hat to Mama as he passed. Papa touched his own hat with the whip, returning the courtesy. "All the vinegrowers are happy this year", he remarked. "No hailstones to damage the grapes."

As they went along, Zoé wondered what Grand-mère had looked like. It was fifteen years ago that she had died in the same little house they were headed for now. Zoé remembered things that happened only in that house: the whirring of the spinning wheel; the warm smell of the crisp ten-pound loaves Mama baked; and the floor boards, how they creaked in the early morning when the sun warmed them!

"Mama," she asked, "why is it that Hubert and Marie-Louise and Jacques and Antoine were born in Grandmère's house, yet Charles and all of us were born at Fain?"

"That's a long question, *chérie*", laughed Mama. "This is how it was. At Senailly I worked as a teacher, in order to support Grandmère."

"What does 'support' mean?"

Mama looked down into Zoé's questioning eyes. "It means to be able to give someone money to help her live nicely. I worked hard. Then, one day, I met your Papa. We fell in love, and he asked me to marry him. After that, we lived with Grandmère for seven years. That's why your oldest brothers and Marie-Louise were born there."

"Then why did you move away from Senailly, Mama?"

"*I'll* answer that", hooted Joseph, who had been listening to the conversation. "Because Grandmère couldn't stand the noise of four wild monkeys in the house. That's why."

Zoé laughed.

Mama tucked in the tail of Auguste's blue shirt and

gave him a kiss on the cheek. The boys poked each other playfully with branches. Tonine sat in the straw watching the kittens, while the wagon jerked along slowly over the bumpy road.

"Oh!" cried Tonine suddenly, "I forgot to give Ninette her milk. Poor little pussy." She lifted the lid of the basket beside her, and out jumped a gray tiger cat. Mama stood up quickly and caught Ninette in her arms. Just then Auguste took it into his head to climb up on his seat and lean over. A sudden lurch; a flash of a blue shirt; then scream after scream. The wagon had plunged into a deep rut, and Auguste lay on the ground.

"His legs! His legs!" Mama cried, as she climbed out and bent over the still, crumpled form. Auguste lay unconscious, arms outspread, his legs under the wheel.

Papa, white-faced, showed the panic-stricken boys how to help him shoulder the wagon and strain to lift the wheel from the crushed legs.

Tonine stood in the road screaming. For a moment Zoé felt stiff and frozen inside. Then, kneeling, she sobbed, "Holy Mary, pray for us! Pray for us! Blessed Mother in heaven, don't let him die. Don't let Auguste die!"

Summer scents came from the woods, the smell of tilled soil. Birds flew swiftly overhead. Only the sobs of the children could be heard, mingled with Zoé's prayer: "Don't let Auguste die!"

2

NOW YOU WILL BE MY MOTHER

IN THE QUIET corner of Burgundy called Fain, life
moved slowly. Farmers worked hard, and their wives
took pride in the cleanliness and order of their homes.
They cooked, washed, fattened poultry, churned butter, and sent their children packing off to school.

Mass was said only on Sunday, and not even every
Sunday, for Fain was only one of the three village
churches served by one priest. Daily family prayers

made every household feel secure against the outer world.

It was said in Fain that the Labouré farmhouse was about one hundred years old, but no one knew for sure. Nine-year-old Zoé loved its gray stone walls, its purple-brown tiling. The beams across the ceiling in the parlor were worm-eaten; outside, the worn cobblestones told of hay carts rumbling over them through the years. From the small window in her bedroom under the eaves, Zoé could see the blue-green valley below. For miles it stretched, dotted with dark church spires among the willows and pines.

Mama too had her favorite window. It was in the square parlor where she sometimes sewed, behind the starched curtains. Other afternoons she read aloud from an old book about the saints.

While the other children were playing hide-and-seek in the big barn, Zoé sat beside her mother cuddling a doll, entranced by the story of Saint Margaret Mary, who, Mama told her, once lived not far away, at Paray-le-Monial.

"Is that in Burgundy, Mama?"

"Yes, *ma petite*", Mama said, closing the book and smiling at her little daughter.

"And Joan of Arc came from this part of France, too, didn't she?"

Mama nodded. "From the village of Domrémy, in Lorraine, near the river Meuse, and . . ." Pausing a moment, Madeleine stroked Zoé's hair. "I don't think

I'll tell you that story again. We can't have tears on a dear little face. That's what happened last time."

"Tomorrow, then? I promise to put my head in your lap and just listen. It's a promise, Mama."

All about the house were reminders of the strong Catholic faith that Pierre and Madeleine Labouré passed along to their children. A framed picture of the Christ Child hung on the parlor wall. In Mama's bedroom stood a statue of the Madonna. One had only to glance out of the window to see the old village church across the lane. Every day Zoé visited the church and spent some time in the little corner that the villagers called the Labouré chapel because Pierre had paid for badly needed repairs.

A year had gone by since the accident on the way to Senailly. Auguste's legs had not been properly set by the doctor, and now it was clear that he would never walk again. Never to chase rabbits or to go scampering over a meadow in spring! Zoé's tender heart almost broke at the thought, and over and over she implored our Lady to console her little brother.

Zoé and the invalid were inseparable. If he wanted something, Zoé must bring it. When one of his brothers answered him, Auguste would shriek, "I want Zoé!"

Once this happened when Papa was working on his accounts in the next room. He called out, "Stop that nonsense! Your sister is busy." Pierre Labouré would have no spoiled children in his family, not even the helpless Auguste. But Zoé was always thinking up some new game that would amuse him.

"Look!" she would say, prancing around wearing Mama's long apron around her waist. Then she would strike a comical pose, holding a birch broom in her hand, tilting up her chin, and pretending to be a queen. The gaiety in her eyes would send Auguste into a trill of laughter.

As Zoé began to do more and more chores around the house, Papa gave her a duty that was to be especially hers. All the others had jobs around the farm, and Pierre felt that Zoé was old enough to take some responsibility.

"I think you are quite capable of taking complete charge of the pigeons", he said in his decisive way. "How would you like that?"

Zoé had always loved to watch the hundreds of pigeons who made their home across the yard in a stone tower. Now she drew herself up, feeling twice as big as she was. "Oh, Papa!" she cried. "I would love it!" Her eyes were shining.

"Then you can begin today", Papa told her.

Zoé loved to have the birds soaring about her, flashing and tumbling with excitement when they saw her coming with their food.

"Mama! Mama! The pigeons know me already", she burst out eagerly a day or so later, as she ran into the kitchen with the empty feed-pan. "They flutter down and perch on my shoulder. One pulled my hair."

"That shows", Mama said, "that they have perfect confidence in you, *chérie*—just as I have."

Such a wave of love for her mother came over Zoé that she threw up her arms for a hug. Mama bent down and kissed her cheek. "God bless my little Catherine Zoé always", she said.

As a summer day is threatened by showers, so a great sorrow was to overshadow the Labouré family. One afternoon in November, Madeleine became ill. By the time the evening Angelus rang, she was worse. The doctor shook his head. Madeleine could not speak, but she smiled at each of her children as they knelt weeping and praying around her bed.

After their mother's death, the children were inconsolable. Papa was almost in despair. "What will I do?" he muttered to himself over and over. "This big house to manage . . . Tonine and Zoé . . . Auguste . . . the other three boys . . . meals for my laborers. . . ." He always ended by throwing out his hands in a hopeless gesture.

"Papa, let me take charge of Auguste", Zoé pleaded, when the family had begun to adjust to their loss. "Let me. . . ."

Pierre looked down into her earnest face and his own softened a bit. "We'll see."

It was kind Aunt Marguerite and Uncle Antoine Jeanrot who helped to settle the problems. "Let the two girls come to stay for a while with us in Saint Rémy", they suggested. Papa gratefully consented.

Marie-Louise had left her home with Aunt and Uncle in Langres and would stay in Fain to help take care of the family. Pierre and Joseph would go to boarding school. Charles had been wanting to go to Paris to learn the catering business; now his father gave him permission to go. "That will leave Marie-Louise with the house and Auguste to look after", said Papa. "That's more than enough for any girl her age to do."

The three oldest Labouré boys were in or near Paris. Hubert was an officer in the French army stationed at Châtillon-sur-Seine. Jacques was in business, and Antoine had apprenticed himself to a pharmacist. The younger children scarcely remembered these older brothers who had been away from home for so long.

Poor Marie-Louise, at the age of twenty, was faced with the huge task of running a household. Until now she had been a schoolgirl with the Sisters of Charity. She had helped her aunt sometimes in the house at Langres, but to be suddenly faced with the task of cooking for the family, and for thirteen hungry laborers besides, was a different matter.

As usual, Zoé was the one to do the comforting. "I can help you. I'll do all the dishes and the dusting–that is, until I go to Saint-Rémy." Bravely she hid the unhappiness that filled her when she thought of leaving home.

The faithful maidservant took over most of the cooking. Still there was the responsibility of housekeeping and ordering when the grocer made his monthly visit with his ox-cart and his account book.

At first Zoé had hoped to find another mother in this older sister whom she hardly knew. But soon she could see that nothing would be the same again. Marie-Louise could never take Mama's place.

One day, when the loneliness seemed unbearable, Catherine Zoé fled to her mother's room, threw herself on the bed, and sobbed. When the tears subsided, she glanced around the room. On a shelf was Mama's favorite statue of our Lady. Zoé slid off the bed and pushed a chair over to the statue. Climbing up to the level of the shelf and taking the statue in her arms, she held it close. "Now, dear Blessed Mother," she whispered, "you will be my Mother." At that moment Zoé promised herself never to cry again about her own dear Mama.

Marie-Louise soon began to pack a trunk for Tonine and Zoé to take to Saint-Rémy. She was weary and disheartened at the turn her life had taken: the loss of her mother, the coldness of her father, who was now withdrawn in grief. For five years it had been understood that she would enter the convent. Aunt and Uncle, the Sisters at school-everyone had been pleased at the prospect. Now, suddenly, here she was with a household to manage, young children to care for, and no hope of a change.

Sensitive Zoé soon noticed her sister's unhappiness. "Tell me, tell me," she begged, "what makes you look so sad, Marie-Louise?" And Marie-Louise, because she had no one else to talk to, confided half-heartedly in the little sister she barely knew.

Nothing could have so pleased Zoé as the thought of a religious vocation in her own family. To spend one's whole life for God, to work and pray and do everything for love of him! Oh, if only Zoé herself could hope for a life like that! But for now she must be content to try to help Marie-Louise.

"Our Lady will help us find a way", she told Marie Louise serenely. "You'll see. Soon you will feel happier." And within an hour Marie Louise was surprised to find that she did feel somewhat happier.

The day the girls were to leave for Saint-Rémy was cold and dreary. As they helped Marie-Louise with the dishes, the mouth-watering aroma of midday dinner still filled the house. "How we're going to miss our two dishwashers!" Marie-Louise remarked to the servant who was stacking pots, pans, and platters.

"I don't want to go to Aunt Marguerite's", said Tonine petulantly. "I'd rather stay here and feed the chickens. No one else can look after them as I do."

Zoé felt the same way. "And what about my pigeons? May I go now and say good-bye to them?" She dashed off, her quick legs carrying her through the kitchen door, across the cobblestones to the pigeon tower.

When she returned, Papa was consoling Tonine.

"Aunt Marguerite will be like a second Mama to you, *chérie*. Besides, Zoé is going with you. She'll take care of you." Zoé never forgot those words. All her life she loved Tonine and mothered her, though she was only two years older than her little sister.

"Aunt Marguerite is here already", cried Marie-Louise, as she hurried to open the front door.

In no time at all the two children were seated in the one-horse carriage with its two big wheels, driven by Aunt Marguerite. The trunk was roped to the back. Zoé's eyes clung to the house and the path where she had so recently skipped along beside her mother, talking and laughing.

The hardest moment of all was when Auguste clung to her dress and would not let her go. "Maybe we'll come home for Christmas", she said, by way of consolation.

The horse started off, and away they went. Soon the two little girls were installed in Aunt Marguerite's house. Uncle Antoine and their four girl cousins gave them a warm welcome.

The Jeanrot home was much different from the farm. The rooms had flowered wallpaper that was faded a little here and there. Between the draped white curtains in the parlor, vases of flowers made splashes of color. A river wound itself unhurriedly at the bottom of the garden. It flowed under several bridges until it was out of sight. A breeze ruffling it made a thousand sparkles in the sunlight.

"What a lovely view!" Zoé said to Tonine as they both looked out of the window.

"Look at that statue of Saint Bernard in the center of the garden", remarked Tonine. "I like that. He looks as if he's blessing us."

Zoé was remembering that her Mama had told her about Saint Bernard and that he too was born in Burgundy.

Just then Aunt Marguerite came into the room, all smiles. Her youngest girl skipped along beside her.

"A special treat for everyone", she cried.

"What is it?" came a chorus of voices.

"Today the candy man comes to the village, selling his wares. Would you all like to buy something?"

What a question! Only at Christmas and Easter did candies appear on the Labouré table. This was indeed a treat for the two girls.

"Oh, la! la!" cried the little cousin. "We must hurry, hurry, hurry before the pink and green nougat is all sold out. Come along, Zoé and Tonine." She took both the girls by the hand and pulled them along with her.

For the first few days the Labouré girls were homesick. In their room on the top floor they clung to each other for assurance. But the Jeanrot cousins were such cheerful companions, they soon made the girls feel at home.

There was so much to see and do that was fascinating. Uncle Antoine's vinegar distillery was a constant source of wonderment. Sometimes he allowed the girls to sit on the pile of sacks containing malt and watch the men shouldering the loads of brown sugar that went to make the vinegar.

"What great big vats!" Tonine exclaimed. "How much do they hold, Uncle?"

"About a hundred gallons", he replied, as he bent down to turn a spigot. It was fun to watch the liquid being released into dozens of containers.

Zoé turned to her sister. "Papa said you were not to ask so many questions and bother Uncle Antoine."

But he only looked up and smiled. "That's the only way to learn", he said, pleased at the interest his nieces showed.

Time passed quickly. . . . It was spring again; the plum blossom misted against the sky.

Eighteen-year-old Cousin Claudine was shocked that the Labouré girls could neither read nor write, but she could not help admiring their devotion. One day Tonine overheard Claudine say to her mother, "Have you noticed the way Cousin Zoé kneels at Mass? So straight, with her hands folded like a saint. I don't think she sees us at all."

Aunt Marguerite Jeanrot sent her two nieces to the village curé's catechism class. It was a new and wonderful experience to Zoé and Tonine, who had never been inside a school before. When class was over, the children would scamper off to play. But Zoé always had other thoughts. She would walk slowly home, relishing every word the curé had spoken about God and his mercy and his love. She lived for the day when she would make her First Holy Communion.

Pierre Labouré had intended his girls to stay at Saint-Rémy only until Marie-Louise had learned to manage the house at Fain. But somehow the time slipped by. Before he realized it, two years had passed.

He sent for his daughters.

3

THE LITTLE HOUSEKEEPERS

C ATHERINE'S DELIGHT at being home was over-
shadowed by the sadness she saw in her father
and in Marie-Louise. Pierre Labouré had become a
silent, brooding man. And, when he was not brooding, the tendency toward sternness, which in the old
days had been tempered by his wife's charm, often rose
fiercely within him. If table conversation did not please
him, he would smash down a strong fist, and something was sure to roll off onto the stone floor and break

into a hundred pieces. If he was working on household bills that seemed too high, he would roll back his chair, slam down the account books, and stomp off to his room.

As for Marie-Louise, she had become a wonderful housekeeper. Planning, cooking, cleaning, laundering-all the things that had seemed so hard were easy now. But the postulancy of the Daughters of Charity seemed to grow farther away each day. Her eyes reflected sadness, sometimes almost despair. Catherine longed to help.

One day, when they had decided that Papa looked quite contented and good-humored as he sat beside the fire, Catherine and Tonine approached him. "Papa," Catherine began, "when I was at Aunt Marguerite's I used to do most of the cooking."

Pierre looked at her for a moment and said only, "Well?"

"So, Papa, I was thinking that Tonine and I could manage this house quite well. We've talked about it. And then . . . then Marie-Louise could enter the Daughters of Charity. She's waited so long." Catherine was almost afraid to look at him.

He looked at the serious faces of his two young daughters and realized that they meant it.

"Marie-Louise's trousseau for the convent has been packed and ready for months", Tonine added in her breathless way. "She's only waiting for you to give your permission."

Pierre Labouré had known for some time that Marie-Louise had a vocation. That was one reason why he had sent for the younger girls. But he still had not decided whether or not they were old enough to take on the responsibilities of the house.

"Well, well," he said now, in a dubious voice and with a measuring look, "you can try if you like. But I warn you, it takes your grown-up sister all her time. And remember, there are many more mouths to feed here than at Saint-Rémy." He shrugged and then added more gently, "You're both too young. However, you can try, as I said. No harm done by it."

Catherine hugged him impulsively. "Oh, *merci*, Papa. *Merci*. I'm quite sure Tonine and I can do a good job. You're going to be very surprised." And off she ran through the wicket to the cherry orchard to tell Marie-Louise the news.

One morning a few months later, Papa came down to breakfast as usual but did not begin to eat. He sat quietly, as if considering something. No one spoke.

Suddenly he sat up straight.

"Well, girls", he said, "I'm satisfied." Then he leaned back in his chair and surveyed his three daughters solemnly. "Yes, I'm quite satisfied."

Marie-Louise looked at her father. "What do you mean, Papa?"

"I mean", he said, stroking his chin, "that I've

decided it's time to let you go to the convent, Marie-Louise."

The girls glanced at each other in amazement.

"Do you really mean it?" asked the oldest girl eagerly.

Pierre took a gulp of coffee. "Did I ever say anything I didn't mean?" he reminded her.

"No, Papa."

"Then listen to what I'm about to say. Zoé and Tonine have proved themselves capable of running this house to my satisfaction. And so you, Marie-Louise, can start making your farewells anytime."

The girls remained silent as they often did when their father made a solemn and unexpected remark, but Catherine felt her heart beating madly with the same joy that Marie-Louise was experiencing.

As soon as Pierre finished his breakfast and had gone out to the fields, the three girls began to chatter at once. Catherine and Tonine both kissed their older sister impulsively. They realized that the long-talked-of parting was now close at hand.

When the day actually came for Marie-Louise to leave, her little sisters waved her off cheerfully as the carriage left for Langres. Afterward, Catherine went upstairs very slowly. She passed the open door of her sister's deserted room. The neatly made-up, empty bed made her feel lonely and frightened.

She stood by her own small window lost in thought. Could she really manage the household with only

Tonine to help her? Then once again she looked up at the beloved statue of Mary standing guard on the shelf. "You have given me a hard task", she whispered. "I am weak and afraid. Blessed Mother, help me."

It was a great burden Catherine had shouldered, and sometimes she felt tired and bewildered. Then she had to remind herself that she was helping Marie-Louise give her life to God. How different that made everything seem!

Catherine made up her mind to cook so well that Papa would not miss Marie-Louise too much. But once she burned the pastry. There was an uneasy silence after she told Papa. "I won't allow waste in any form", he said through tight lips. Catherine knew that he was very angry. She would have to work harder and pray harder to our Lady, who had managed the household at Nazareth.

Catherine attended to Auguste like a mother hen with a chick, and the shy child was delighted to have his gentle sister at home again. She washed the clothes in a wooden tub, beating them with a bat. There was bread to be kneaded, the pigeons and poultry to be fed.

Tonine followed Catherine like a shadow. Her particular duties were to make the beds, keep the furniture and floors shining, and help with the dishes, but somehow she always managed to be where Catherine was, because she could not bear to be without her.

One morning the girls were filling baskets with

bread and cheese to take to the laborers in the fields. Catherine was exceptionally quiet, and of course Tonine had to know why. "What are you thinking of, Zoé? You seem so quiet and worried. Tell me!" But Catherine only smiled and gave Tonine a playful hug.

"Nothing at all, my pet. I just feel a little quiet today."

Each laden with a great pitcher of wine and a basket covered with a white cloth, the two girls put on their cloaks and walked to the door.

Catherine paused in the doorway and turned toward the small bed with its curtains drawn back. Here Auguste lay all day. "We won't be long, *chéri*." With love in her eyes, she smiled at the little invalid. "I'll make you a cake this afternoon, sweetheart. And when Tonine brings in the eggs I want you to help me count them."

A rosy flush spread over the pale cheeks. Catherine had made him believe she couldn't count them without him. "Will there be raisins in the cake and sugar on top?"

"We'll see", Catherine said, but Auguste knew from the twinkle in her eyes that there would be both raisins and sugar.

Catherine could not tell Tonine why she was quiet because she did not know herself. All she knew was that she could not stop thinking of her First Holy Communion, which she was soon to make. Each day she walked a mile and a half to the stone church of Moutiers-Saint-Jean for instructions. This was the principal church of the three villages, the place where the pastor of the three resided. It was a beloved spot to Catherine, who had often heard Mass there with her dear Mama and her brothers and sisters.

Often Catherine rose before dawn to walk to the Hospice de Saint Sauveur, conducted by the Daughters of Charity in the same village of Moutiers. It was here that the priest said his daily Mass. As Catherine's sabots clacked along the deserted country road, her happiness would mount. Soon, soon, the great day would be here when she would approach the altar for the first time.

At last the day came. Catherine knelt before the altar in the church at Moutiers-Saint-Jean as the stained-glass window, bathed in morning sunlight, sent a warm glow over the heads of the First Communicants. Catherine felt as if she were no longer on earth, so deep was her joy.

"I'm going to Mass every day from now on", she announced a few days later.

Tonine protested. "You can't do that. What about the housework? And suppose it's raining? You can't walk all that way.

Nothing would stop Catherine. "I shall get up at four o'clock and be back before you begin to get breakfast." And so she did.

When Catherine began to fast every Friday and Saturday, Tonine scolded. Catherine explained that she wanted to make this little sacrifice. Tonine was not satisfied. Finally, she threatened, "I shall tell Papa."

"Very well," Catherine replied, "tell him."

Tonine went straight to her father. "Papa! Papa! I've something to tell you."

She told him the story, and he agreed that she had been right to inform him. "Send Catherine to me at once", he commanded.

"I've already given one daughter to religion," he explained when Catherine stood before him, "and that is enough. A girl of your age is not asked to fast twice a week."

"Please, please don't forbid me, Papa", she pleaded.

"Well, I won't exactly forbid you. I only ask that you use the common sense God has given you. There's a great deal of work to be done here and it is your duty to keep up your strength."

Catherine continued to fast, and, since her health did not suffer, the subject was never mentioned again. More and more she began to hope that the day would soon come when she could give the rest of her life to God.

Whenever someone told Pierre how hardworking his two girls were, he was proud. But once or twice he wondered if he was being too severe with them. One day he came in from the fields and said:

"Catherine, I need your help outside. The soil has to be prepared in the vegetable garden."

Both girls with sleeves rolled up were preparing to cook. Catherine's voice rose. "But Papa, I promised to make Madame Jeanneau one of my best cakes. I hate to disappoint her."

"A promise is a promise!" put in Tonine, her voice charged with meaning.

With his hand still on the kitchen door, he said in a softened tone, "I don't blame the old lady for wanting one of your cakes. I enjoy them myself." He paused a moment, thinking. "It has just struck me that you girls haven't had much fun lately. Would you like to enter the baking contest at the Fête?"

Could this be true? The girls looked at each other in amazement. Tonine gasped. "Do you mean it, Papa?"

He nodded. "I'm planning to take you both on opening day. I thought that perhaps you'd both like to bake something. It would be more fun for you that way."

Catherine drew a great breath. "My entry wouldn't be good enough. The Fête at Montbard? Why, everyone knows that only the best cooks compete."

"Well, you can try", Pierre said.

Tonine's mouth was a big round O. Catherine idly sifted flour through her fingers into a bowl.

When Pierre went back to the fields and the girls had recovered from their surprise, they talked about Papa's suggestion. The idea of baking something for strangers didn't appeal to Catherine. When you put in ingredients for someone you knew, she thought, a certain amount of love went in with them.

"Suppose you won a trophy, Catherine. Wouldn't that be splendid? Papa would burst with pride."

"You try, Tonine. I'll help you. I'd like you to shine before the other girls in the village. You could learn to make *babas*. It might be fun."

Catherine pulled out a drawer in the kitchen dresser and began to hunt for something. Moments later she found it: an old box made of wood, with faded pictures of Paris painted on the lid. "I remember Grandmère used to keep her favorite recipes in this", said Catherine.

Not being able to read was such a handicap, but Catherine had a remarkable memory. She would get a neighbor to tell her the recipe, and she would remember it.

Tonine's eyes sparkled. "I can't believe we're going to the Fête. It's too good to be true. But I'd be afraid to try to make *babas*."

"Oh, they're not too difficult, *chérie*." Catherine glanced at the clock and said, "Oh, I must hurry with this cake. I forgot Papa had asked me to help him!"

The very next day Tonine began to learn how to make *babas*. The first batch went up in smoke, and there was no way of hiding the thick black cloud that waved in the sunlit kitchen. "I hope Papa doesn't come in now", she wailed.

"No use worrying," said practical Catherine. "If it's God's will that we get a scolding, it will happen." She opened the windows.

Scarcely had Tonine uttered the words than the door opened and Pierre came in. She smiled at him a bit, hoping to take the edge off his anger. "I'm afraid I burnt the cakes. . . ."

"Oh, well," said Pierre, "keep trying." He glanced around the kitchen. "Did I leave a rake here this morning?"

"No, Papa. Not here."

Pierre went out as quickly as he had come in.

"Well," gasped Tonine, "Papa must be very anxious for us to bring home a prize from the Fête. I expected a lecture on the sin of waste."

The goings-on at Montbard gave the girls of Fain-les-Moutiers much to talk about. Anticipation rose to great heights. Each girl discussed what finery she would appear in at the Fête. Some of them were going to wear lace bonnets that were packed away carefully for such occasions as fêtes and weddings.

The Labouré girls were content to have neither ribbons nor earrings. The fun of going was quite enough for them—but secretly Tonine hoped Papa would let them stay for the dance in the evening.

At last the great day dawned. Catherine awoke early. She kept saying, "Hurry, Tonine, hurry. We mustn't keep Papa waiting!"

The dishes were washed, the pigeons fed, and everything was in order before they left the farm in the wagon. As they drove along, the trees were yellow with laburnum. Others spilled out into spikes of white lilac. A glorious day!

"Why, I never did hear such a noise!" cried Tonine as they neared Montbard. "Isn't this exciting?"

Although it was still quite early in the morning, the booths were all set up and doing quite a business. The Fête was being held in the marketplace, right in front of the church.

While Papa chatted with some of his friends, the two girls went up to the smiling woman at the food booth and asked if they were too late to make entries in the baking contest.

"Why, no. Lots more entries to come. And you two are just the nice sort of girls we want to win the prize."

She entered their names in a book and admired the cake and the *babas* as she took them. The woman was fat and good-natured. She looked so comical with a pencil sticking out of the big bun on top of her head. "Why, bless me," she exclaimed, "there's more din than a thousand starlings could make."

Great bustling was going on all around.

Farmers and their wives strolled about. Some people must have brought all their grandchildren with them. An ox was lying on the grass, half asleep and chewing his cud. A small terrier barked impudently at him. A man came by selling balloons.

Suddenly there was music. A young man was playing an accordion. When the girls found their father, he was talking to some of his friends. "Come, join us in some wine", they were urging him.

When the men had been seated, Pierre asked, "Do you know when they are going to judge the baking contest?"

"At twelve noon", someone told him, trying to make himself heard over the mingling of noises.

Pierre told the girls, "I'll be here at this table at a quarter to noon. Meet me here, and we'll watch the judging."

"Yes, Papa", said Catherine.

"I'm hungry, Papa", Tonine whispered.

Pierre said, "There are all kinds of things to eat here." He thrust some money into her hand.

Before she had thanked him, she let out a whoop of joy. She had seen some of her friends and was eager to explore the Fête with them. When Pierre said yes, she was off in the twinkling of an eye.

Catherine turned away from the table to avoid the insistent gaze of a young man seated opposite her father. She did not enjoy his obvious admiration, and she hurried away in the direction of the booths.

Never before had she been alone in a crowd of noisy people. She couldn't help feeling timid and drew back when a man tried to sell her toys. "Step up for jack-in-the-box. A wonderful surprise for children. Observe, jack pops up when I open the lid . . . *Voilà.*"

Catherine wished she could buy several of the toys on display for Auguste. But she had only enough money for one. In the next booth sat a very old woman making pillow lace. A crowd had gathered around her. How such gnarled fingers could weave delicate lace butterflies was a miracle. Hundreds of bobbins were arranged on a pillow resting on her knees. By looping threads over a number of pins arranged in a pattern, she slowly created lace.

Catherine felt lonely and lost. She wished Tonine were with her.

She was managing to work her way out of the crowd when she felt something pulling at her skirt. Next moment she was aware of a small hand clasping hers.

"*Maman . . . Maman . . .* lost."

Catherine looked down into the eyes of a small boy. His face was tear-stained and dirty.

"There, there, *mon petit*", Catherine whispered, taking the toddler up in her arms. She wiped the tears away. "We'll go to all the booths, and you look for your *maman*."

After a while the child began to cry again. "Poor little love", said Catherine, and, seeing just the right toy to please him, she bought it. The shiny tin whistle made the tears cease immediately, and the price was small enough so that she could buy a flute for Auguste as well. She understood the child's feelings, for she herself felt lost in the crowd. How could any mother be so careless? Catherine asked herself. No one came forward to claim the lost boy.

Now they reached the place where the lucky spinning wheel was drawing dozens of people. No *Maman* there. At that moment the Angelus rang out from the steeple.

"Bells", said the child pointing a chubby finger in the direction of the sound. "Bells!"

All bargaining stopped to do honor to our Lady.

A metallic thud told Catherine that the child had dropped the whistle on the cobblestones. She was startled by a voice behind her. She looked around and saw it belonged to an old priest who was talking to the child, his face filled with kindness. His hair fell upon his shoulders. He wore his cassock.

"Mademoiselle, I think this is the young man who has wandered away from his Mama", he said, retrieving the whistle.

Catherine smiled. "Yes, *mon père*. I've been hoping to find his mother."

"She is one of my parishioners. If you will wait one moment, I'll bring her here."

Within a few minutes mother and child were reunited. Catherine hurried away in a happy daze. She almost knocked over a boy who held up some sprays of dried lilies of the valley. Each had a verse attached.

"I'm sorry", she gasped.

"Buy a token of future joy?" he asked.

Catherine shook her head. Suddenly she remembered her promise to return to her father before twelve. The Angelus had rung long ago. She had completely forgotten about the contest.

When she reached the table where Pierre and Tonine were sitting with friends, Tonine gave her a warning glance. "Where did you go, Catherine?"

The expression on her father's face was forbidding. "You're late!" he snapped.

"I'm sorry, Papa."

Tonine looked upset. "You won first prize, Catherine. We were so proud. But . . ."

If I won, why is Papa so angry? Catherine asked herself.

Someone's name was being called out. A girl rose and made her way to the judge's stand. *Monsieur le Maire* pinned a red ribbon on her dress, and everyone clapped.

Papa was scowling. "You know how I feel about punctuality, Catherine. You were not here when your name was called. You lost by default to the second-prize winner. I had hoped to be proud of you. I suppose you were star-gazing as usual."

"I'm sorry, Papa." She felt miserable, wishing her father would not scold her in front of so many listeners. Better let Papa think her careless than go into explanations, she thought.

"What about your *babas*, Tonine?"

Her sister made a wry face. "Oh, some nasty creature

made hers better than mine." Then she added with a shy grin that gave her a dimple, "I'm only joking. I really didn't expect to win."

A wave of tenderness for Tonine broke over Catherine. "Are you happy, *chérie?*"

"Oh, yes", she said fervently. "It's all so wonderful!"

The crowds were beginning to thin out. Although it was still early, most of the farmers and their families had driven a long way and had to be up before cockcrow.

"We'd better be turning toward home", said Pierre. "We mustn't leave Auguste too long."

Tonine didn't want to leave. "Look! Papa, look! There's a juggler. Oh! I wonder what he's going to do with the rabbit. Could we . . . Papa, could we . . . ?"

"Step up close, little lady", cried the showman, beckoning to Tonine. But she knew it was hopeless. No use at all. When Papa said "home", he meant it.

No one had much to say on the way back. Only the thud of the horse's hoofs broke the silence. The music and the shouting faded away. But the day would never be forgotten.

"We had a good time, Papa", said Tonine. Pierre replied, "A change doesn't hurt anyone. You girls should get to know more people."

Papa meant to be kind, but Catherine knew that making more friends or seeing new things could never make her happy. To be a Sister was her only idea of joy. Marie-Louise understood that.

Auguste's welcome home was delightful. His pale face broke into a smile of joy when Catherine presented him with the toy flute she had brought him. He succeeded in putting it to his lips and making a hollow chirping sound.

"I can make a tune!" His unaccustomed fingers seemed to fall in the right holes on the instrument. Toot! Toot! Toot!

"Now, you watch me", said Pierre taking the flute gently from Auguste and playing a simple song.

"Why, Papa!" exclaimed Tonine. "I never knew you could play."

"Nor I", said Catherine.

Pierre's heart warmed at their admiration. "Well, that's the last surprise of the day. We'll all have to work twice as hard tomorrow to make up for lost time. To bed now, everyone."

"But Auguste hasn't seen my lovely bracelet. And I haven't given him my present yet", Tonine protested loudly. "Here it is, *chéri*."

Madame Jeanneau was tying a scarf over her head. She was about to leave. But curiosity got the best of her. "Oh, am I missing something?" She came hurrying back.

When Auguste opened Tonine's present his smile broadened to a grin. "Oh! Oh! A picture book."

On the front cover was a picture of a galleon in full sail. Both Catherine and Tonine, who could not read, would have a wonderful time using their imagination.

What tales they could weave to keep the little invalid happy!

"Auguste has been an angel all day, Monsieur Labouré", said Madame Jeanneau. "Angels are always rewarded!" She walked over to the door. "Well, good evening, everyone."

"Thank you", said Pierre as she closed the back door.

Later, after the girls had said their prayers and were in bed, Tonine fell asleep almost at once. But Catherine told herself, I've seen more people and more new things today than ever before. Oh, yes, I enjoyed them all. But more than ever I know these things are not for me.

4

ONE DAY YOU WILL COME

T HE DAILY ROUND of duties went on until Catherine was nineteen. Marie-Louise was already superior of the Daughters of Charity at Castelsarrasin. Such a rapid rise in the religious life filled her younger sister with happiness, perhaps mingled with a spark of natural envy.

Pierre Labouré was beginning to show signs of age. He constantly complained, but Catherine bore his sharp tongue without a word. One day, when he had been especially irritable, Tonine turned to Catherine, who was preparing vegetables. "Why don't you get married?" she asked. "I would, if I had all the admirers you have." She began to count them off.

"Hush, hush, Tonine, *chérie.*" Catherine touched a playful finger to her little sister's lips. "I've not changed my mind. I've promised myself to our Lord. Some day I know he will give me the chance to enter the religious life."

Not long after, Papa told Catherine that a well-to-do young man from a neighboring village had asked his permission to pay court to her. "How do you feel about it, child?"

Without a moment's hesitation Catherine answered. "I'm sorry to disappoint you, Papa. I do not wish to marry."

Pierre nodded gravely and gave no argument. He seemed quite relieved. "Well," he said, taking down his long pipe from the rack and filling it with tobacco, "that suits me too. I've no wish to lose my daughter."

Catherine watched him light his pipe, take a few puffs, and then walk out into his own room to read the newspaper. He always smoked when he was contented.

As time went on, Catherine's attraction for the religious life became stronger and stronger. Only in prayer could she find consolation. Slipping away whenever her work allowed, she knelt in the Labouré chapel beneath the old painting of the Blessed Virgin. There, she felt closed off from the rest of the world.

One night Catherine had a puzzling dream. She saw herself sitting in her usual place in the chapel. An elderly priest whom she had never seen before was saying Mass. He had a grave, gentle face, a short pointed beard, and on his head a black skull cap. When he turned around, he looked at Catherine very seriously, and she could not take her eyes from his face.

Before going to the sacristy after Mass, he beckoned to her. Catherine was afraid and left the chapel hurriedly. In her dream she went to visit an invalid before returning home. When she entered the room, she saw the same priest again.

"You flee from me now," he said, "but one day you will be glad to come to me. God has plans for you; do not forget it."

When Catherine awoke, she experienced a feeling of great happiness, but she did not know why. She lay in bed thinking and wondering. What did it mean? Never would she forget the priest's face, and yet she had no idea who he was.

When she was twenty-two, Catherine decided to open her heart to her father. She would tell him of her vocation and ask his permission to leave. Tonine had become an accomplished housekeeper, and Papa would be well taken care of. Over the years Catherine had shown her love for him in a thousand ways. He is a good Christian man, she thought. Surely he will not refuse me.

Pierre Labouré was poring over his accounts. Books, papers, and discarded quill pens showed that this was not the best time to approach him. He looked up. The familiar frown puckered his forehead.

"Papa, I've something to ask you."

He laid down his pen, leaned back attentively in his chair. "Well, Catherine?"

Catherine sat down. She was cool and precise, her hands folded in her lap. "Papa," she began, "I want your permission to go away. I want to enter a novitiate. I'm sure I have a vocation."

"What? What do I hear?" Her father jumped up, his face crimson with rage. "Most certainly not! Why . . . I've never heard . . ." His anger choked him. Striding back and forth, his hands behind his back, he shouted at his daughter. "If you had asked permission to marry, I would gladly have given my consent. But to see you go off to a convent . . . certainly not!"

Catherine recoiled from his anger. Her heart was beating so fast that she could scarcely breathe. It was as if a bolt of lightning had struck her. "It's all I've ever asked", she managed to say. "Surely you can't refuse?"

"Enough!" He stopped pacing up and down, his mouth a hard line. He pointed a finger at her. "My girl," he said, "I not only can refuse, but I do. The answer is . . . no!" He strode out of the room banging the door behind him. Nothing broke the stillness but Catherine's sobs.

Pierre's anger lasted several days. Tonine begged her sister to be patient. "Papa will change his mind and let you go."

He did change his mind, but not in the way Tonine expected. It came about through a letter from Charles Labouré. He wrote about the sudden death of his young wife, just as he had bought a small restaurant.

"Poor Charles! Poor boy!" Papa murmured after he had read the letter aloud. He knew only too well what it meant to lose a dearly loved wife. His eyes softened with sympathy for his son.

When Pierre came down to breakfast the next morning, determination had replaced the sorrow on his face. Catherine glanced across the table at Tonine, wondering if she also had noticed the change.

"I've been thinking", Papa told them, "about Charles' letter. I've decided, Catherine, to let you go to Paris to help your brother in his restaurant."

Pierre expected a blush of happiness to cross Catherine's face. Instead she turned pale with horror and found herself tongue-tied.

"Well?" thundered the former Mayor of Fain in his most official voice. "Haven't you a word of thanks?"

Silently Catherine stared at the tablecloth. Her father went on, "I shall write to Charles today and tell him to expect you as soon as possible."

The thumping of her own heart was all Catherine

could hear. Her throat was dry. "I'm ready to do whatever you say, Papa", she whispered in a trembling voice.

"That sounds more like an obedient daughter!" Pierre drew from his pocket some crisp notes. "Take these. Next market day buy some material for new clothes. You can make for yourself whatever is needed. We can't have Charles feeling ashamed of you."

With that he pulled back his chair noisily and went out into the fields to work.

The two girls fell into each other's arms. "If you were leaving to enter the novitiate, I would be happy for you", said Tonine. "But the great city of Paris! . . . You'll be miserable."

The day of departure drew near. The village girls were jealous of Catherine's good fortune and could not understand her reluctance to leave. One of her pretty cousins came with Aunt Marguerite from Saint-Rémy to see her off. Her aunt presented her with two pairs of long black stockings, hand-knitted. "It's cold in Paris", she warned.

Catherine was touched by everyone's kindness, but inside she felt sick with loneliness. Constant prayer was her only comfort. God saw into the depths of her heart and found there obedience.

The squeak of wheels and the thunder of many hoofs told of the arrival of the diligence. The family was standing on the flagstone porch, waiting, Tonine already in tears and Aunt Marguerite trying to be cheerful.

Catherine looked sadly at her father, hoping for an affectionate word, a half-promise that she might still hope for the convent. But when he said his good-bye, there was no remorse in his voice. Pierre Labouré was a proud man.

In her black cloak and hood, Catherine stood biting her lips as she watched one of the farmhands tow away her portmanteau, with the big umbrella strapped to it. She waved good-bye as she settled herself in a seat beside the other passengers. The driver took his place. With a crack of the whip the four horses started the clumsy carriage off again. A cloud of dust arose, and she was gone.

Catherine tried hard to control her tears as the carriage bumped along. Silently she implored the help of our Lady on that long journey that would end in the great bewildering city of Paris.

To feel the warm welcome of an older brother in a crowd of strangers was an overwhelming joy. It had been thirteen years since Charles had left Fain for Paris, yet brother and sister knew each other at once. The Labouré features were unmistakable.

Exhausted by fatigue and fearful of her new life, now that the first joy of reunion was over, Catherine was almost afraid to raise her eyes as she and Charles rode through Paris. Her brother talked continuously, pointing out places of interest, asking a hundred questions about the family. Catherine felt a cold fear in the pit of her stomach. Such great buildings! Such wide streets! So many people!

Nor was Charles' restaurant in the least what she had expected. It was more like a hole in the wall, with its long table and wooden benches. The kitchen was dark and stuffy. Catherine felt choked from the first moment she entered it.

After one week of waiting on Charles' customers, Catherine wondered how she could go on. The men who came to eat teased her unmercifully.

"Watch me", one soldier said, winking at his companion over his coffee. "I'll make the country mouse talk!" Catherine was coming from the kitchen carrying a pile of plates. The rowdy soldier waited until she approached the table, then suddenly thrust out his foot. Catherine almost fell. There was a general roar of laughter.

Although her cheeks burned with anger, Catherine did not say a word. She only looked from one to the other. Something in her eyes silenced them.

"You mustn't mind their coarseness", Charles told her later. "They don't come here to learn manners, you know." He paused and put down the glass he had been polishing. "But one thing does surprise me, Zoé. Since you have come, I've noticed they curb their language. You seem to have reformed them a bit."

In spite of her courage, poor Catherine often

broke down and wept when she was alone in her narrow room under the roof. Charles was not blind to her unhappiness and wrote to his oldest brother, Hubert, for advice. Chevalier Hubert Labouré came immediately from Châtillon-sur-Seine. In the little room behind the restaurant, he and Charles discussed their sister. Hubert was in favor of taking her back to Châtillon, as his wife had suggested. "But you know how severe Papa can be", Charles reminded him. "He sent her here, and this is where he wants her to be."

Before Charles could reply, Catherine appeared at the door carrying a big, shiny coffee urn. Her two brothers rushed to help her.

"What a lovely surprise!" cried Catherine, seeing her oldest brother in his dashing uniform for the first time. "So much gold braid! Such great shining epaulettes, and a sword dangling from your belt! How wonderful you look, God bless you, Hubert."

"Zoé, let me look at you! You were so little when I saw you last." Hubert stood smiling in disbelief at his grown-up sister.

As the three sat down, Hubert said, "I've brought a message from Jeanne, my wife. She wants you to stay with us at Châtillon. She runs a school for young ladies there. We've plenty of room and a beautiful garden, and everything you could wish for." His voice was warm and kind.

"But . . . Papa? He will be . . ."

"Let's leave everything to Jeanne", Charles broke in. He smiled knowingly. "Our sister-in-law is a very clever woman. She can get Papa's consent to let you go, if anyone can."

Months went by while the letters passed between Paris, Fain-les-Moutiers, and Châtillon. But at last Pierre Labouré was won over. He agreed that at Jeanne's school Catherine might learn to read and write and maybe study some arithmetic too.

The house where Jeanne lived was large and fashionable. Once again Catherine found herself in a totally new world. The streets bustled with activity. Smart carriages took ladies for airings, and children played at bowling hoops.

Inside the house people came and went. A maid wearing a starched apron over her long black dress and on her head a cap with streamers hanging down her back showed people upstairs. A long carpeted hall led to Jeanne's private reception room. There she interviewed the parents of prospective pupils.

Catherine felt miserably out of place in rooms where the draperies were made of blue silk and the furniture was upholstered in brocade.

"Now, don't get up early, Catherine", said Jeanne kindly. "Take a good rest. You've been working much too hard."

But to lie unhurried in a soft bed while the morning sun shone through the windows was impossible.

Catherine rose at her usual hour and spent the time in prayer. She was almost afraid to go downstairs, for fear of disrupting Jeanne's household arrangements. Sometimes she stood hesitantly outside her bedroom door, waiting until she felt the right moment had come to appear in the breakfast room.

The pupils were haughty girls from the highest society in Burgundy. When they looked at Catherine, her ears, cheeks, and chin felt red and hot, because she was aware that they thought she had no right to sit at the same table with them. Longing for convent life, she was bewildered by such extravagant surroundings.

The situation had its difficulties for Jeanne also. Until Catherine arrived, she had not known that her young sister-in-law could neither read nor write. But she cheerfully bought new clothes for Catherine and put her in the dancing class with the other girls. There were lessons on how to hold a fan, how to curtsy gracefully. The girls giggled at Catherine's awkwardness. The dancing master grew angry. Catherine was in an agony of misery.

Jeanne, seeing that she had made a mistake, hastened to take Catherine out of the class. "I'm ashamed of my students", she apologized sadly to her sister-in-law. "I would never have believed that they could be so rude. From now on I shall teach you myself."

Already Jeanne Labouré had grown to love the girl whom she felt God had placed in her care. The good schoolmistress was well known at the Hospice of

Charity in Châtillon, where she was so close to the Daughters of Charity that she might almost have been one of them. One day Jeanne took Catherine with her and introduced her to some of the Sisters. Just to be on that holy ground filled Catherine with peace. She felt as if God at last were drawing her closer.

Soon after this first visit, as Catherine waited one day in the parlor to see the superior, she chanced to look at a picture on the wall. Surely . . . surely, she thought, going to look at it more closely, why . . . yes! It was the portrait of an aged priest with a pointed beard and a black skull cap. He seemed to be smiling at her. Her heart gave a leap as she recognized the priest in her dream who had beckoned to her.

Catherine was so excited that as soon as Sister Superior had greeted her, she asked eagerly, "Sister, could you please tell me whose portrait that is?"

"Of course, my dear. That is our Father Founder, Saint Vincent de Paul."

Catherine said no more, but a great peace enveloped her from that moment. She was sure now that God wanted her to be a Daughter of Charity. On the way home she confided in Jeanne, who had already guessed her sister-in-law's yearning.

"We'll do everything possible to help", she told Catherine. "Hubert and I will consider it a privilege to provide your trousseau."

Catherine had to wink back the tears. "How good you are to me, you and Hubert. How good!"

Jeanne embraced Catherine warmly. "I feel sure that the Sisters at the Hospice would welcome you. But there is still one difficulty to overcome", she warned.

"Yes, I know," Catherine replied heavily. "How are we going to get Papa's consent?"

As before, it was Jeanne who tackled the problem. She approached her father-in-law in such a diplomatic way that old Pierre Labouré gave his consent. But, he added, he would not give one thing toward Catherine's clothing and dowry.

No complaint against her father passed Catherine's lips, but she was deeply hurt by his stubbornness. She need not even have asked his permission, since she was twenty-three, but she wanted her obedience to be perfect.

On January 22, 1830, Catherine left to make her postulancy in the Hospice de la Charité at Châtillon. Fourteen years had gone by since she had chosen Mary for her mother. Looking back, she realized what great grace had been given her. She had tasted hardships and had been granted strength to bear them.

Deep in her heart she was convinced that by entering the Hospice she was doing God's will. She had practiced austerities daily and was now willing to break her own stubborn spirit into fragments that she might be received as a Daughter of Charity. Sometimes she fought hard against the doubts and misgivings that beset her. Fully aware that she had many shortcomings to correct, Catherine always prayed to Mary for help, knowing that one's mother never refuses.

Though only a postulant, still called Mademoiselle Labouré and wearing her own simple secular clothes, Catherine was allowed to observe the full religious day of the Daughters of Charity. All her life she had waited for this; now at last she was happy.

The superior put Catherine in the charge of her assistant, Sister Séjole. Gentle and motherly, Sister Séjole had a reputation for discerning the qualities of the young postulants, and in Catherine she immediately saw extraordinary holiness.

Catherine had found a wonderful friend in Sister Séjole, who soon set about to teach her new postulant to read and write better. "Never mind now, my dear", she would say when Catherine was momentarily discouraged. "We shall work together, you and I, and soon you will be reading and writing as well as any of them." Touched and pleased, shy Catherine could only hope that Sister Séjole sensed her gratitude.

Catherine did her work well, yet simply. She loved everything about the life at Châtillon and never tired of hearing about beloved Monsieur Vincent, her Saint Vincent de Paul, who had gathered together the first Daughters of Charity to care for the poor and sick. If some of the Sisters thought Catherine cold and distant, there were others who recognized the goodness beneath the shyness.

When the day came that she could read a letter from

her sister Marie-Louise without any trouble, Catherine was overjoyed. Sister Séjole found her pupil sitting in a corner beaming over the letter. She smiled affectionately at Catherine's gratitude. "No, no, my dear. Don't thank me. It was you yourself who did it. And it *was* a bit of a penance, wasn't it?"

In April 1830, the time came for Catherine to leave Châtillon forever. An elderly Sister was to accompany her to the Motherhouse at 140 rue du Bac in Paris, where she would begin her novitiate. To Catherine and to Sister Séjole the parting brought a moment of pain. Yet each had her own consolation. Sister Séjole knew even then, as she later revealed, that Catherine Labouré was different, that God had chosen her for some special purpose. For Catherine the parting meant that she was moving closer to the religious life for which she yearned.

The elderly Sister waited patiently while the farewells were said. For her it would be the last journey. She was going home to the motherhouse to spend her last days.

"Good-bye, and a happy novitiate", Sister Séjole whispered. "We shall miss you sorely."

"Pray for me", was all Catherine could say. With one backward loving look she joined her companion and turned toward Paris.

5

DOORWAY TO SANCTITY

To ANYONE ELSE but Catherine, the welcome she received on her arrival at the motherhouse in Paris would have seemed a cold one. A few words, a smile half directed at her elderly companion, and that was all. But the swelling of her heart told her that here in this hallowed place she was to find fulfillment. For Catherine there were no doubts, no feeling of panic.

Once past the long narrow alley that led from the imposing front doorway to the novitiate, the old Sister companion paused to sit down and catch her breath. A few moments later, she introduced Catherine to the mistress of novices, Mother Martha.

She was kind. "I'm sure you would like to make a visit to the Blessed Sacrament first", she said, showing the way to the chapel.

Catherine's impression as she knelt before the beautiful altar was a feeling of homecoming. Here, at the very heart of the community, she once again made a gift of herself to God.

"Lord, here I am! Dear Mother, I'm so happy!"

As she knelt, the hardships she had surmounted to reach this goal melted away. They were only stepping stones toward perfection.

Having made her visit, she returned to the mistress of novices. "We shall call you Sister Labouré for now, you know", Mother Martha said, kindly but firmly, as she showed Catherine her sleeping cubicle. "Your name in religion will come later, when you receive your habit."

Catherine could hardly keep from singing the next morning when she put on the old-fashioned black dress of the novice, the white pointed fichu and the white headdress, the same costume the peasant girls had worn in Saint Vincent's time, two hundred years before. When in chapel she would wear a black taffeta hood as well.

Almost as soon as she arrived at the motherhouse, Catherine had the great joy of assisting, along with the other "Little Sisters", as Saint Vincent had called his first daughters, in a glorious religious ceremony. The body of Saint Vincent de Paul was to be honored— Saint Vincent, the saint of her dream, whose gentle smile had made known to her that one day she would come to him as an obedient daughter!

Since 1793 the body of the saint had been hidden. Several times it had been removed to places of safety during the Revolution and the Reign of Terror that followed. Later, when the Sisters were allowed by the government to resume their community life, the holy remains found a place of honor in their house on the rue du Bac. Now the Vincentian Fathers had built a beautiful new church of Saint Vincent around the corner from the Sisters' motherhouse, and of course that was where the beloved body of Saint Vincent was now to lie.

On April 25, 1830, the remains were carried in solemn procession from the Cathedral of Notre Dame, where they had lain in state for a month, to the church of Saint Vincent.

Catherine's joy was almost more than she could bear. Only a few days after her arrival at the novitiate, to be a part of this glorious religious pageant was more than she had ever dreamed of.

The singing of the *Te Deum* was heavenly. Never before had she heard anything so beautiful. Nor had she seen so many nuns, priests, and brothers chanting together as the procession wound through the narrow streets.

Was this the same Paris? Catherine remembered the quarrelsome voices she had heard when she went marketing for Charles. She had not forgotten the bad language that rose from the underground passages and dark alleys. It had seemed as if God had been banished from that part of the city.

But today, how different! It was as if the souls of the Parisians had blossomed forth once again in a burst of religious exaltation. All Paris had turned out to witness the procession, of which Catherine herself was a humble part.

Old soldiers, pastry cooks, housewives, and children watched respectfully. Even the pickpockets mingling among the crowds hesitated to pursue their trade. Men doffed their hats and women blessed themselves as the relics went by.

Amidst all this homage to Saint Vincent, lover of the poor, rescuer of orphans, comforter of the sick, there walked another saint, eyes cast down, unaware of the immense graces that were to be hers.

As flowers open to the sun, so Catherine opened her heart to Saint Vincent. She prayed for the graces she needed for herself. She asked the blessing of heaven on her beloved France. She was dazzled by the procession of clergy in glittering vestments; the soldiers in parade dress, marching and swinging their white gloves in perfect rhythm; the heavenly chanting; the sight of the eight hundred Daughters of Charity. And yet, impressed as she was with this outer display, Catherine's joy was even deeper, because she knew that Monsieur Vincent had but a simple heart, like her own. He was the son of a farmer, as Catherine was the daughter of one. A great love of France was common to both.

The solemn procession and Translation of the remains marked the beginning of a novena in honor of Saint Vincent. Each morning, for nine days, a pontifical Mass was sung in the church of Saint Vincent. Each afternoon a novena service was held, and at all of these functions the Sisters and novices from the rue du Bac were present. More and more fervently Catherine prayed to her spiritual father.

One day, after Catherine had returned to the Sisters' chapel from the novena service, she was looking toward Saint Joseph's altar, where a relic of Saint Vincent was enshrined. Suddenly, above the shrine, she saw the heart of Saint Vincent.

Catherine was startled and bewildered. Then a feeling of security came over her, and she understood, without being told in words, that this heart symbolized peace, calm, and the happy union that existed between Saint Vincent's communities—the Vincentian priests and the Daughters of Charity.

The next day Catherine saw the heart again. This time it was fiery red, and she understood that it symbolized the warmth of charity that the community would extend throughout the earth.

The third time the heart appeared, it was the color of a deep red rose. Catherine was filled with a great sadness as she understood the message: she herself would have much to suffer, and there would be a change in the government of France. A voice told her: "The heart of Saint Vincent is deeply afflicted at the sorrows that will befall France."

Throughout the novena the heart appeared several times, and on the last day Catherine heard the voice say that God had provided that Saint Vincent's double family would not perish, in spite of future hardships and perils.

Catherine Labouré knelt in the darkened chapel after the last vision, wondering what to do. She was just a simple country girl who knew nothing of such things as visions. All she wanted was to love God and our Lady and Saint Vincent and to do her work well. But now it seemed that Saint Vincent wanted something special of her. She would have to tell her confessor. He alone could help her. But would he believe her story? Would anyone believe that an unworthy novice like herself had been singled out?

Father Jean-Marie Aladel—confessor, chaplain, and spiritual director of the Sisters—was only six years older than Catherine. A fervent Vincentian, he was severe with himself, strict with others, and cold in his manner. Catherine trembled at the thought of telling him. If only she knew him better it might not be so difficult, but she had been to confession to him only once.

When she found herself in the dark of the confessional, she plunged into her story as quickly and matter-of-factly as she could. If Father Aladel was surprised, he did not show it. He brusquely told the novice to think about other things and control her imagination. "Only then will you know peace."

But Catherine knew no peace. She lived in an agony of suspense, all the while trying to perform her duties and learn what was expected of her.

God was soon to show his young novice even more amazing favors. At Sunday Mass about a month later, during the Gospel, our Lord himself appeared to Catherine. He was robed as a king, in crown and regal garments, a cross at his breast. As she gazed upon this vision, she suddenly saw the crown, cloak, and cross fall to the ground. Catherine trembled. This vision surely must mean that something would happen to the king, Charles X. Had not Saint Vincent foretold a change of government? If the king's power fell, it would bring to an end the power of the Bourbon family, who could trace their ancestors through history as far back as Charlemagne.

Catherine pondered the meaning of these things

and decided that she must try to approach Father Aladel once more. Perhaps he would be able to understand the meaning of the vision that filled her with so much fear.

But she met with the same rebuff. This time the young priest was determined to stop this talk of visions. Young novices were always thinking they had had some extraordinary spiritual experiences, and one had to be firm. He simply told Catherine a bit impatiently that she was to stop telling him such nonsense and to get hold of her emotions before they carried her away.

Poor Catherine left the confessional determined to obey Father Aladel and forget the visions. She would keep herself very busy and pray even more earnestly to our Blessed Mother for guidance.

In the silence of the novitiate, Catherine waited, content to pray and leave the rest to God.

6

OUR LADY'S VISIT

THE STREET SOUNDS of the sprawling city of Paris were subsiding. Only a few shouts, some off-key singing, and the occasional rattle of wheels over the cobblestones broke the silence

It had been a stifling day, and on this night of June 18, 1830, the Sisters and novices had gone thankfully to bed. Because tomorrow would be the feast of Saint Vincent, they had been extra busy.

The air became cooler now, and a faint breeze stirred in the dormitory. But the Sisters and novices in their curtained cubicles slept without benefit of the cool air. They enjoyed the sleep of the physically tired.

Just before bedtime, Mother Martha had talked about the love of the saints with such warmth that Catherine could not rest. Never before had she felt such a deep love for her Blessed Mother. Never before had she longed so earnestly to see her. This thought filled her mind until a great feeling of peace came over her. It was the kind of peace she had known after the dream of Saint Vincent.

She was so filled with the ardent desire to see the Blessed Virgin that she fell asleep at last, certain that her prayer would be answered.

When she had been asleep two hours, a light suddenly appeared from somewhere in the dormitory. She was surely dreaming. No! There really was a light. Catherine heard her name called.

"Sister Labouré! Sister Labouré!"

She sat up, opened the curtains of her bed, and saw a child dressed in a long white gown, carrying a lighted candle. He had the face of an angel.

"Come to the chapel", he said. "The Blessed Virgin awaits you."

I must be dreaming, thought Catherine, and hesitated.

The child, seeing that she was uncertain, reassured

her. "Do not be uneasy. It is half past eleven, and everyone is asleep. Come. I am waiting for you.

She hesitated no longer. Dressing quickly and putting on her black taffeta hood, she was ready to follow the child.

How her heart was beating! "I am going to see her", she murmured to herself. "I am going to see the Blessed Virgin!"

They hurried across the dormitory to the hallway and down the stairs to the chapel. The heavy wooden door, always locked at night, flew open at the touch of the child's hand.

Catherine gasped. The chapel was a blaze of light, as if a thousand candles were burning. The brightness almost dazzled her eyes. It was as if the Christmas Midnight Mass were about to begin.

The child stopped in the sanctuary and stood by a chair that was covered in rose-red damask. It was used by Father Aladel when he gave his talks to the Sisters. Catherine knelt, suddenly afraid to look up.

She was sure the Blessed Virgin was not there, and for a moment she trembled in fear. The moments were passing. How marvelous that not one of the Sisters had come down to see why the lights were on! The child stood waiting.

At last the little messenger spoke. "Here is the Blessed Virgin."

A sound of rustling, as if someone were walking in a silk dress, reached Catherine's ears. She looked up and saw a lady come down the altar steps and seat herself in Father Aladel's chair.

For a moment, a breathless moment, Catherine wondered if she were being deceived. Was this lady a dream? Was she imagining?

The child reassured her. "This is the Blessed Virgin", he said. When Catherine still hesitated, the messenger spoke in a different voice, the stern voice of a man.

The doubt flew away as fast as it had come. Catherine felt her cheeks flushing in shame. She lifted her eyes and beheld the most beautiful face she had ever seen. Unable to utter a word, Catherine fell to her knees and rested her hands in the lap of her Blessed Mother. She had no fears. It was the same gesture she would have used if she were talking to her own mother.

"My child," began our Lady gently, "the good God wishes to charge you with a mission." She went on to warn Catherine that she would suffer every kind of mistrust in carrying out the mission, but that she must think of the glory of God while she was doing it. And she would have the comfort of always being certain of what God wanted her to do.

"You will be tormented", our Lady went on, "until you have told him who is directing you. . . . Tell with confidence all that passes within you. . . . Give an account of what you see and hear . . . of what I tell you, and of what you will understand in your prayers."

The young novice hung on every precious word that was spoken to her as she looked into the eyes of our Lady.

"The times are very evil", Mary went on. "Sorrows will come upon France. The throne will be overturned. The whole world will be upset with miseries of every kind."

As our Lady spoke of these calamities, a look of infinite sadness crossed her face. Catherine could see the pain that the sins of man caused her. "Come to the foot of the altar", she said, pointing to the exact spot. "There, graces will be shed upon all who ask for them."

Every precious word rang in Catherine's heart. Never before had such a wonder happened. Many times our Lady had appeared in the world, but never had anyone knelt before her and rested her hands in Mary's lap. Yet, this was happening to a lowly country girl from the little village of Fain-les-Moutiers.

Now our Lady spoke of the Vincentian Fathers and of the Sisters of Charity. "I love to shed graces on your community", she said. "It pains me that the rules are not observed. Tell that to him who has charge of you, even though he is not the superior."

Catherine trembled at the thought of trying to tell Father Aladel about her vision and what our Lady had told her to do. He certainly would never believe her.

"When the rule is strictly observed once more," our Lady promised, "another community of Sisters will ask to join this one."

This prediction was fulfilled nineteen years later. Elizabeth Ann Seton, a young American widow, had become a Catholic, against great opposition. In spite of seemingly insurmountable difficulties, she had established a community of Sisters. In 1849 Mother Seton's Sisters of Emmitsburg, Maryland, united with the French Daughters of Charity.

Not a candle flickered. The flowers on the altar, so beautifully decorated for tomorrow's feast of Saint Vincent, filled the air with faint perfume. The heavenly child waited.

Sister Labouré thought that the Blessed Virgin had finished speaking. But she had something more to say, and she said it with tear-filled eyes. This was more than Catherine could bear. Our Lady spoke of the suffering to be endured by other communities. "There will be victims among the clergy of Paris. The cross will be treated with contempt; they will hurl it to the ground. Blood will flow. . . . Monseigneur the Archbishop will be stripped of his vestments. The whole world will be in sadness."

When she had made her predictions and answered Catherine's questions, our Lady vanished as quickly as she had come.

Now only the candles reflected in Catherine's face. Her Blessed Mother was gone. What should she do about the candles? She wondered who would snuff them out. What would the Sisters say if there were none left for the feast day?

She looked at the child who was still standing there. He would know what she should do. He smiled at her and turned toward the great wooden door of the chapel. Catherine rose and followed him.

Up the narrow stairs they went again, Catherine following the little figure in the dazzling white gown. When they reached the side of the bed and she turned to thank him, he too had faded away. She was alone once more.

When she was calmer and better able to gather her thoughts together, she realized that the beautiful child in the shining garment was her Guardian Angel. Had she not prayed to him to watch over her ever since she was a child?

She listened now as the bells pealed from the many church towers in Paris. Two o'clock! Our Blessed Mother had talked with her for two hours! It had seemed but a few minutes. Two hours more and it would be time for the convent to stir. The feast day was already here.

Catherine had no thought of sleep. She sat up with her hands clasped, reliving every moment of those two hours.

Next day she could think of nothing but the message our Lady had told her to deliver. How could she tell Father Aladel? Already he was impatient. What would he say to this miracle, even more difficult to believe than what she had told him before? But our Lady had said, "You will be tormented until you tell him."

The waking-up bell sounded through the dormitory. Soon the Sisters and novices would be filing two by two into the chapel to begin the special devotions for the feast day. Catherine wondered absently whether the same angelic hand that had lighted the candles last night had put them out.

Everything in the chapel was the same as before. The candles looked as if they had never been lighted. The chair looked just as Father Aladel had left it. Catherine wished she could tell all of them that our Lady had come. She had smiled upon the Sisters of Saint Vincent!

Catherine lived in confusion and dread until the day Father Aladel came to hear the Sisters' confessions. As she knelt in the darkness of the confessional, she could not quiet her thumping heart. Pressing the palms of her hands together hard, she tried to gather strength to begin.

Father Aladel once again listened to an extraordinary story told by a young nun who certainly seemed to be a sensible practical country girl. He listened attentively and thoughtfully but showed no sign of being convinced.

Within a month our Lady's prophecies were fulfilled. On July 27, 1830, rioting broke out all over Paris. Mobs armed with muskets looted churches, shouting, "Down with the priests! Down with the king!"

One group went to Saint Lazare, the house of the

Vincentian Fathers, to ransack and burn it. But our Lady protected both the Vincentians and the Sisters of Charity from the wild band, just as she had promised. The mob left after pulling the cross from above the front door and destroying it publicly.

In the great silence of a retreat at 140 rue du Bac, Catherine prayed at the foot of the altar where the Blessed Virgin had promised graces. In the Vincentian house around the corner, Father Aladel followed the news of swiftly-moving events and realized with a strange and troubled feeling that he was a witness to prophecies fulfilled.

7

"HAVE A MEDAL STRUCK!"

Paris had settled down once more. For the
novices in the rue du Bac, life went on, undis-
turbed by the bloody three-day revolution. Only the
professed Sisters had braved the riotous streets on their
errands of charity.

The old king had retreated to England, and Louis-
Philippe came to the throne. For Parisians life went on
peaceably in the great sprawling city.

Leaves were falling in the seminary garden at the rue du Bac. The hot summer had gone some weeks before, and now Catherine and a group of white-bonneted novices worked each day at raking the leaves that carpeted the ground.

Catherine had asked permission to take care of the twisting vine that canopied the white statue of Mary with the Holy Child. This beautiful work of art presided over the recreations and the laughter of the young girls, who knew that a cheerful heart is a gift of God.

Whether in the garden, or scrubbing a floor in the great kitchen, Catherine's thoughts kept going back to the sweetest moments of her life, the moments when she knelt at the feet of the Blessed Virgin. And when Father Aladel did not seem to believe her, she heard again in her heart our Lady's words: "You will be tormented . . . but do not fear. Have confidence."

When the silence of evening filled the convent, Catherine's thoughts sometimes turned to the Burgundy countryside. She would close her eyes and visualize the white mist coming down from the far-off mountains, the autumn leaves crunching underfoot, the tinkling of nearby sheep bells. Then she would be filled with gratitude for the marvelous way God had brought her to Paris and to the novitiate.

At half past five on Saturday evening, November 27, 1830, the Sisters and novices were making their meditation in the half-darkened chapel. White bonnets and starched cornettes caught in the flicker of candlelight made a picture of spiritual peace. As always, Catherine was thinking of our Lady, longing for the other Sisters to share with her the joyous knowledge that our Lady had favored their own chapel with her presence.

Tomorrow would be the first Sunday in Advent. Thoughts of our Lord's coming at Christmas filled the hearts of the Sisters. Then . . . Catherine's heart gave a great leap. Out of the silence came the sound she had heard once before, a faint rustle of silk, the whispering of our Lady's gown as she walked.

Scarcely able to breathe for joy, Catherine saw before her in the sanctuary the Blessed Virgin, shining, radiant, beautiful. She stood on a globe and was wearing a soft gown. Sister Labouré noticed every detail of it.

The color was like the whiteness of dawn. The neckline was cut high, the sleeves plain. On her head was a delicate white veil that fell gracefully to her feet. Beneath the veil was a lace fillet, which lightly bound her hair.

In her hands the Blessed Virgin held a golden ball. Her eyes were raised heavenward, as if she were offering the ball to God. Then, quite suddenly, there seemed to be jewelled rings on her fingers. From these, precious stones flashed like rays of light. They illumined the globe so brightly that Catherine could no longer see our Lady's feet.

Mary looked into Catherine's eyes. Her lips did not seem to move, but out of the stillness came a voice.

"The ball that you see represents the whole world, especially France, and each person in particular."

Catherine was so entranced that she was completely unaware of the other novices kneeling on the Gospel side of the chapel or of the professed Sisters across the aisle. She knew only that the rays of light from our Lady's fingers were growing more and more dazzling.

Again the voice came. "These rays symbolize the graces I shed upon those who ask for them. The gems from which the rays do not fall are the graces for which souls forget to ask."

The golden ball vanished from our Lady's hands, and her arms opened in a gesture of love. The light bursting from all sides like a fountain of glory fell upon the white globe at Mary's feet. Then, as if drawn by a heavenly hand, an oval frame took shape around her. Written within the frame in letters of gold were the words: O Mary, conceived without sin, pray for us who have recourse to thee.

Again Mary addressed Catherine: "Have a medal struck after this model. All who wear it will receive great graces. They should wear it around the neck. Graces will abound for persons who wear it with confidence."

Then, in order that Catherine should see the other side of the medal, the whole vision revolved. In the

center of the oval was a large "M". This was surmounted by a bar that had a cross on it. Beneath the
"M" were the heart of Jesus, crowned with thorns,
and the heart of Mary, pierced with a sword. Encir-
cling the medal were twelve stars, perhaps representing
the twelve apostles. As Catherine watched this great
spectacle, she took in every detail of the other side of
the medal. Then the vision was gone, like a candle
suddenly extinguished.

This, then, was Sister Labouré's mission, which our
Lady had announced on the night of her first visit to
the chapel. Now Catherine understood.

How she reached her place at the long refectory
table she never found out. She had no recollection of
walking out of the chapel, nor did she remember saying grace. Food was certainly in front of her, but how
it got there she did not know.

Mother Martha gave her a reproving frown. She
hoped that this new novice, who seemed like such a
sensible, country girl, was not going to turn into a
dreamer. Catherine wondered what she had done, or
perhaps had not done. Her mind was in a whirl.

When Catherine knelt again in the confessional, she
was fearful but determined. This was a direct message
from heaven, a command from the Mother of God.
Father Aladel *must* listen!

Once she had understood his doubts. After all, it did
sound like a daring piece of vanity to say that one had

seen the Mother of God. But now it was different; now she had a message to deliver. And yet it seemed that our Lady failed her every time she faced this stern judge. He listened to her, but with no real interest. When she asked that he promise never to reveal that she was the Sister who had seen our Lady, he readily agreed. But he did not promise to have the medal made. Catherine could do no more.

After she had left, Father Aladel sat quietly, troubled and wondering. This novice was a simple girl, hardly able to read or write. Surely she could not have imagined the details she had described.

Could it be, then? Could it possibly be that the Blessed Virgin really had appeared to Sister Labouré?

As time went on and Father Aladel did not act, the Lady of the Medal came again and again to stand reproachfully before Catherine. Each time the novice obediently told her confessor that our Lady had come again.

"I had to tell her that nothing had been done, that you would not listen to me." Catherine raised a tearful face. "I even told her, Monsieur, that she had better appear to someone else, because no one would believe me."

"What!" gasped the priest. "You are a wicked wasp to say such a thing!"

Strangely enough, Catherine was no longer afraid. She knew that she had shocked Monsieur. Perhaps that was what our Lady had meant her to do. Perhaps now, at last, he would act.

But months passed, and Mary's wishes were not obeyed. Whether preparing pails of vegetables, washing stacks of dishes, or scrubbing or cleaning, Catherine's unfulfilled mission was ever before her. It was her daily martyrdom.

As the novices came to the end of their novitiate, a feeling of excitement filled the air. Retreat was over, and during recreation the girls chattered like birds in a treetop. It was a time of happiness and of great hopes for the future. There was the possibility of being sent to any part of the world to work for the glory of God.

"I hope I go where there are lots of children", remarked one novice.

"Oh, yes", agreed Catherine. "I expect you come from a large family like mine."

Her mind flew back to her own childhood. What fun she and Tonine had had, pretending to be knights and dragons and ladies in distress, just to amuse Auguste. How he used to laugh!

Another novice stood gravely by, listening to the others. "What are you hoping for?" Catherine asked.

"I would like to care for old people. It must be terrible, being old and alone."

"A leper colony in the South Seas for me", said another. "That's what I want. To be missioned to some faraway place, like French Guiana . . . oh, that would be wonderful!"

Already they were beginning to feel the joy of those who, loving the poor and the sick, are loving God. Catherine's dream was about to be realized. She would belong entirely to him, to serve him in his poor.

It was a happy day when Sister Labouré, now to be known as Sister Catherine, exchanged the white coiffe for the graceful cornette, symbol of the Daughters of Charity. The soft white fichu was replaced by the starched collar that fastened at the throat and crossed over a little at the ends.

One thing remained the same, the apron. "That", said Mother Martha, "is the sign that we are servants, Servants of God."

Catherine did feel a little strange at first, wearing her winged headdress. But oh, the joy of knowing that her beloved Saint Vincent had wanted that kind of cornette, copied from the peasant girls of his day and approved by him for his "Daughters". Her spirits soared as she pictured herself walking the streets of Paris, a faded umbrella on her arm, carrying a basket of food and medication to the sick. She could hardly wait for her assignment, and yet, one thing bothered her.

"Suppose I am sent abroad, to Africa perhaps?" she asked herself. "How then can I accomplish my 'mission', if I am not able to speak with Monsieur Aladel?"

When assignments were given out, Catherine found that she was being sent to the Hospice of Enghien, only six miles outside of Paris. She would work in the kitchen of this home for aged men who had served the royal Bourbon family. *"Merci, ma mère"*, said Catherine, smiling.

Mother Superior looked at her in some surprise. Seldom had she seen such a radiant smile on the face of any girl assigned to work in a kitchen. She could not know the real cause of the smile reflected in those dark blue eyes which had looked upon the beauty of the Madonna.

Catherine, hurrying to the chapel, saw the hand of God in her assignment. Not in faraway lands was she to fulfill her mission, but in Paris. And another blessing—Father Aladel would still be her confessor. He was the regular confessor at the Hospice.

"Dear Blessed Mother," she whispered, kneeling at Saint Joseph's altar, where she had seen the heart of Saint Vincent, "thank you for arranging everything. Thank you for making it possible for me to keep urging Monsieur Aladel to have your medal struck. How tired you must be of waiting!"

On February 5, 1831, Catherine left the novitiate where she had spent nine happy months. It was difficult to bid good-bye to the place where her Guardian Angel had sought her out on that glorious summer night. This place was, to her, the dearest spot on earth.

On the east side of Lake Montmorency, surrounded by beautiful linden trees, the Hospice of Enghien sheltered fifty old men. It had been founded by the Duchess of Bourbon in memory of her son, the Duke of Enghien, who had been cruelly shot to death in the trenches of Vincennes Prison during the Terror. The hospice was connected by a long garden to the House of Charity of Reuilly. The Sisters of both houses gathered together in the chapel at Reuilly, and the superior of Reuilly was superior of Enghien as well.

Catherine, smiling under her white cornette, now began her lifetime of work as a Daughter of Saint Vincent in this old house. "Of course," explained Sister Superior Savart, "you won't remain in the kitchen forever. After a while you will probably be in the clothes room, and then will come the care of the old men." Sister Savart paused as if to emphasize her next words. "The men are not easy to care for, Sister Catherine. You must have great patience. Many of these old retainers of the Bourbon family have seen better days, and they don't let you forget it!"

Catherine had no fear of any work that might be assigned to her. Whatever it might be, she would put her heart into it. She wanted her obedience always to be perfect. Now, as she entered the great kitchen for the first time, she prayed: Lord, my work is beginning. Let me never waste a precious moment of it.

For five years Catherine was to peel and scrape vegetables, carry coal and wood for the fires, and polish the great soup kettles. The kettles reminded her of the kettles at the farm at Fain, but those had belonged to her father, while these belonged to God. They must shine like mirrors.

Everything Catherine did was a prayer, but sometimes her heart was like a leaden weight. Weeks passed in which she almost despaired of her mission. When would the wishes of the Blessed Mother be fulfilled?

On a happy visit to the rue du Bac one day, soon after her assignment to the hospice, Catherine was kneeling in the chapel. Suddenly, over the high altar, she saw Our Lady of the Medal, just as she had appeared five months before. Catherine stared enraptured and, at the same time, sorrowful, because Father Aladel had not acted.

"You will see me no more," said the Blessed Virgin, "but you will hear my voice in your prayers." Catherine knew perfectly well that our Lady was not pleased that the medal had not been struck. Time and again after that, Catherine did hear her Mother's voice, just as she had promised. "But, my good Mother," Catherine explained once, in an agony of distress, "you know well that he will not believe me."

When Catherine told this to Father Aladel, he leaned forward in his chair. "And what did she answer?" he asked eagerly. "What did the Lady say then?"

"She said," reported Catherine, " 'Never mind. He is my servant and would fear to displease me.' "

The words struck deep in Father Aladel's soul. *He is*

my servant and would fear to displease me. Never before had he been so stirred.

After Catherine had gone, Jean-Marie Aladel sat alone in the confessional and wondered. Perhaps, after all, he ought to go to see the archbishop.

While Catherine was quietly going about her duties, Father Aladel, in the company of a priest from his house to whom he had confided his problem, went to the archbishop's residence. Being careful not to mention Catherine's name, he told Monseigneur de Quélen about one of his penitents, who had been favored with visions.

A smile lit up the aristocratic face of the archbishop as he listened to what Father Aladel had to say.

"The Blessed Virgin asked that the medal should be struck. She asked for it several times", said the priest, visibly worried. "I feared it might be the work of the devil." He made a puzzled gesture. "I don't know what to do."

The archbishop thought for a few minutes; then his eyes took on a melting warmth. "I see nothing contrary to the Church's teaching in this medal", he said. "I myself have always had a special devotion to the Immaculate Conception of our Lady. And, so long as you are convinced of the piety of your penitent . . ."

"Oh, yes, Monseigneur, I am."

"Then," said the archbishop, "I give my permission for the medal to be struck."

Father Aladel sighed. His agony of uncertainty was

over. The responsibility now rested with the kindly archbishop, known for his wisdom.

"What greater manifestation of God's providence could we ask for, my dear Father Aladel, than a vision of our Blessed Lady in the chapel at the rue du Bac? When the medals have been engraved, Father, I should like to have one."

Unaware that the longed-for time had come, Catherine worked quietly on. Today she was rolling out pastry. Oh, if only her *chaussons-de-pomme* would turn out as well as they used to at the farm! Madame Adelaide d'Orléans, sister of Louis-Philippe and benefactress of the hospice, was coming to visit. On occasions like this, when she brought supplies of new linens, extra care was taken over the preparation of food. Madame Adelaide liked apple dumplings. Papa had liked them too. Catherine thought often of her father. How strange it was that in the end he had been so hard; she had always loved him so.

As Catherine bent over the table, her sleeves pinned up, an extra blue-checked apron covering the front of her habit, Father Aladel sat in his study thinking of the day he had called a Sister favored by heaven a "wicked wasp."

8

THE POWER OF THE MEDAL

JUST ABOUT THE TIME Father Aladel made up his mind to see an engraver about the medal, a dreadful outbreak of cholera swept through Paris, and all action was abandoned, except the care of the victims. The Daughters of Charity nursed the sick and the dying until they themselves were ready to collapse. Into the tenements they went, seeking victims of the dread disease, many of whom lived only a few hours, deserted by their fearful relatives.

Father Aladel worked tirelessly, directing the Sisters' charity. When at last the terror was over, they realized that not one of the good Sisters had caught the disease. It was impossible not to see in this the protecting hand of God.

Father Aladel was now free to turn his attention to the medal. On a beautiful day in May, he sought out the engraver Vachette, on the second floor of No. 54, Quai des Orfèvres. The name of Vachette would go down in Catholic history as the man who played a part in giving the Miraculous Medal to the world.

A shaft of spring sunshine brightened up the old workshop as Father Aladel opened the door. Monsieur Vachette was peering into a magnifying glass, examining some of his work. He looked up, pulling down his spectacles from his forehead at the same moment, and saw the figure of Father Aladel. A smile of welcome crossed his face, and soon the purpose of the visit was being discussed.

"Every detail must be done perfectly. There must be no mistake", said the priest. "Remember, it was our Lady herself who designed the medal." Father Aladel found himself trembling with excitement. He who had taken so long to believe in the medal was now in a hurry to have it struck.

Monsieur Vachette listened attentively. Then he wrinkled his brow, took off his velvet cap, and scratched his head in perplexity. "It's not going to be easy, Father", he said. "But if our Lady wants it . . . she will help me."

"Think, my good man. Think of the graces that may be yours", Father Aladel urged. "People may be blessing you all over the world."

Now it was the old engraver's turn to be excited. "Tell me, Monsieur, how many would you want?"

"Twenty thousand."

Monsieur Vachette's bushy eyebrows shot up. "Twen . . . ty thou . . . sand?" He was almost speechless. Never before had he received such an order.

"Before long, you will find yourself a rich man, Monsieur Vachette," said Father Aladel, "in more ways than one."

With a grateful lift of the heart, Catherine's director realized, on his way back from the Quai des Orfèvres, that he had been an instrument in starting something that was to gladden the world. Our Lady herself had asked for it.

On June 30, 1832, the first medals were delivered. Father Aladel himself went to Enghien to present some to Catherine. She studied them carefully, turning them over and over in her hand.

"Are you pleased?" he asked.

She looked up and gestured vaguely. "Oh, Monsieur, of course this could not begin to show how beautiful she was. But how happy I am to see it at last! Now," she concluded in her simple, determined way, "the medal must be propagated." When she was alone, Catherine was overcome with joy. At last, at last, our Lady's medal had been made!

There was great enthusiasm at the rue du Bac over the medal Father Aladel introduced. The Sisters knew only that our Lady had appeared to someone within the walls of the motherhouse. That much information had been circulating for some time. But what everyone wanted to know was: to which Sister had our Lady appeared? Excitement and curiosity filled the rue du Bac and Enghien houses. *Who was the favored Sister?* Through it all, Catherine kept her secret, even though she was often suspected and even rudely questioned by some of the curious Sisters.

Catherine cherished every bit of news about the medal. Pope Gregory XVI had placed one at the foot of the crucifix on his desk. Archbishop de Quélen had carried one in his pocket when he went to visit a dying excommunicated priest. Unrepentant at first, the man had a miraculous change of heart and was received back into the Church before he died peacefully.

So many hundreds of favors were attributed to the medal that Archbishop de Quélen assigned a learned priest to the task of examining and verifying the wonders. After some months, the priest made his report to the archbishop.

"Monseigneur," he explained worriedly, "we cannot possibly publish all these manifestations of the power of the medal. They would fill a book!"

"Then," replied the archbishop, "we shall have a book."

Thousands of copies of the report were sold. New editions had to be printed. The marvelous propagation of the medal was a miracle in itself.

Nearly two years passed by, while Catherine worked quietly at Enghien, before the archbishop took his next step. He ordered a canonical inquiry to determine the validity of the visions. Father Aladel was called to testify and was told to bring with him the Sister of the apparitions.

Poor Catherine! She had kept her secret so well. How could our Lady ask this of her? She simply *could not* discuss the visions with the priests appointed to the council.

"My dear Sister," urged Father Aladel, "surely it is not too unreasonable a request. His Excellency has even said that you may wear a veil over your face if you wish."

"Please, Monsieur Aladel . . . I beg of you not to ask me." Catherine shook her head and pressed her hands together to steady them. "I couldn't. . . . I couldn't. . . ." She looked so troubled at the thought of it all that Father Aladel understood. His whole sympathy was with her. He explained the situation so effectively that the archbishop immediately withdrew his request that Sister Catherine appear.

Catherine was touchingly grateful. "Oh, thank you, Monsieur. Thank you." Then she admitted, with a shy smile, "I could not have answered any questions even if I had been asked them, Monsieur Aladel."

"But . . . why not?"

"I have forgotten every detail of the apparitions", was the serene reply.

At first, the astonished priest could not believe his ears. But later, when he pondered Catherine's words, he realized that our Lady had come to her aid in keeping the secret by giving her this temporary lapse of memory.

Though the Sister of the visions was still unknown, the canonical inquiry of Paris praised her virtue and wholeheartedly concluded that the Blessed Virgin had indeed communicated to that Sister the message of the Miraculous Medal. "The medal is of supernatural origin", was the conclusion reached. "The wonders worked through it are genuine."

Now Catherine could be content. Two months later, still unknown, she quietly began her life work of caring for the old men at the Hospice of Enghien.

Although she had been warned by the Superior that some of the men were almost impossible to manage, Catherine loved her new work. Anything she did for them was repaid in the devotion they showed her.

"We've never had anyone so kind to us before", said one of her charges, as she tucked him into bed and arranged his pillow. There was something in her touch that soothed even the most disagreeable of them.

Before her men went out for a walk, Catherine

always made sure they were neat and tidy. "Ah," she would say with a smile, as one of them walked toward the door, "you mustn't go out until I've brushed your coat. And your boot laces! They aren't done up. You'll fall over them." Nothing would do but she must bend down and fasten them for him.

For forty years Catherine took care of her old men, feeding them, nursing them through illnesses, and scolding them when they did not behave. When one old fellow refused to curb his bad language, Catherine simply told one of the Sisters with a chuckle, "Next time he wants to go for a walk, he'll find that I've hidden his overcoat until he learns to behave."

While she sewed buttons on the old men's coats or darned socks, Catherine sometimes let her thoughts wander to her loved ones. Tonine was engaged to be married to a fine man, Claude Meugniot. Catherine was glad that Tonine would have a home and family of her own; she had cared for her father so faithfully until his death. But if there was happiness in Catherine's heart for Tonine, there was grief for Marie-Louise, the beloved and admired older sister who had led the way to Saint Vincent's home. She had left the religious life and was living in Paris as a schoolteacher. Catherine prayed constantly that God would bring her back to her religious vocation.

Catherine was so busy at the hospice that each day was over before she realized its passing. Many times a day she crossed from the Enghien house to the Reuilly orphanage, never failing to stop to say a Hail Mary at the statue of our Lady in the garden.

She loved to feed the chickens. In the poultry yard she was always reminded of her childhood in Fain, when the pigeons had encircled her head and perched on her shoulder.

Now that the Miraculous Medal was becoming known everywhere and its power acknowledged by the clergy and laity alike, Sister Catherine reminded Father Aladel about another request of our Lady.

"You remember, Monsieur, that she asked that a statue be made of her—not as she appeared on the medal, but as she was in the beginning of the vision, holding the globe in her hands, offering it to God."

"Ah, yes, Sister, but these things take time, you know. We should be grateful that the medal is being propagated."

"But she asked for the statue too, Father", Catherine prodded. The determination of old had not weakened. She would plague Monsieur Aladel until he consented to our Lady's request.

Still another of our Lady's requests had been for the establishment of the Confraternity of the Children of Mary. But in this too, Father Aladel was slow to act. When at last he announced to Catherine that he was working on the formation of the confraternity, she turned her joyous dark-blue eyes upon him.

"Oh, Monsieur! How wonderful!" she cried. "Think how the young people of Paris will benefit.

Those dreadful crime-ridden districts near the Gare de Lyon! Such terrible things, so much evil. . . ."

Her face became troubled as it always did when she thought of the devil's work.

"Well, Sister Catherine," replied Father Aladel, "I'm afraid Paris will have to wait."

"Wait, Monsieur?" she echoed, suddenly overcome with anxiety.

"Yes." He spoke abruptly, but a faint smile lit up his frank eyes. "You see, the first group in this confraternity is going to be formed in Beaune."

This was happy news for Catherine. She had heard a great deal about the Hospice de la Charité at Beaune. It was not far from where she had been born, on the Côte d'Or. One of her father's laborers came from there, she remembered.

"Oh!" she cried with a happy sigh, "in the very heart of Burgundy. What more beautiful place could you find anywhere?"

Once again Catherine was to be disappointed: ten years were to pass before the voices of girls praising Mary in the confraternity would be heard in Paris. The procession solemnly took place in the parish of Saint-Louis-en-ville, and Father Aladel himself was the director.

Catherine, though not officially connected with the Children of Mary, was overjoyed whenever she heard of a new group being formed to do honor to Mary Immaculate. She wanted to be a source of encouragement to new members and made it a loving gesture to chat with each one who joined the organization at Reuilly.

"I want you to love Mary as much as I do", she told them. Her assurance went further. "Believe me, dear children," she said, "Our Blessed Mother will look upon you from heaven and smile because you have chosen to honor her."

Pope Gregory had died, and now the new pontiff, Pius IX, gave his blessing to the newly-formed association of the Children of Mary. Slowly, but surely, our Lady's missions were being accomplished. Catherine did not reckon the expense. Only the joy counted.

Sometimes Catherine was able, through divine revelations, to know the thoughts and temptations of those around her. One day she was walking in the garden at Enghien and noticed the troubled face of a young Sister sitting under a tree. Though a book was open on her lap, she was not reading.

"Little one," said Catherine going up to her, "you are pondering something evil in your head, aren't you?"

Startled, the girl looked up. "Oh! But, how . . . how did you know?"

Catherine sat down beside her. "What is troubling you, child?"

The girl began. "When I came here, it was to nurse

the sick. But instead, I've been given teaching to do. I hate teaching!" She stopped a moment, ashamed of her outburst. A very new Daughter of Saint Vincent, she had not yet learned the secret of obedience.

Although Sister Labouré gave her a look of encouragement, the girl continued to clasp her hands in a gesture of anguish.

"I just can't face those orphans. There are too many of them. Besides, I've never taught before." Tears ran down her cheeks and fell into her lap. "Yes, I am planning to return to my family."

"Listen, *ma petite*," Catherine reassured her, "if you stay another year, I promise you one thing. You *will* persevere in your vocation. You will also pass all your exams."

The next day, when they met, Catherine knew she had averted a crisis. A happy smile lit up the girl's face. What had been foretold did come about. The young Sister remained at her work, finding great joy in teaching orphans. Whenever she met Catherine, she would give her a smile, as if to say: "Thank you, thank you."

Now, from all sides, came news of conversions through the power of the medal. Sometimes the ecstasy within Catherine's soul was such that she felt overcome by it, so much happiness that she could scarcely bear it.

Then would come sorrow. Auguste had died at the age of twenty-two, Tonine wrote. His death had been gentle and smiling. Fain was hundreds of miles away, but infinitely near to Catherine were the days of her childhood: the farm hidden among the meadows and the vineyards, the stone archway that formed the entrance to the farmyard, and across the cobblestones the great brick tower for the pigeons.

Now, with Tonine's letter in her hand, she closed her eyes. Why, there was Auguste's childish voice, helping her count the eggs! It was years since she had seen him. She could not think of him as a man. To her he was still the innocent child whom God had now taken to himself.

Tonine now was free to marry Claude Meugniot. She had waited patiently to settle in a home of her own. In 1838, they were on their honeymoon, and after that they settled in a cottage in the village of Vizerny.

"You'll be happy to know, dear Zoé," Tonine wrote, "that our brother Antoine has bought the farm. None of us wanted it to go to strangers. . . ." Ah, that is good, thought Catherine.

In 1842 an event occurred that drew international attention to the Miraculous Medal. A great deal of excitement had been stirred up in Europe by the bitter opposition to Catholics of a wealthy and influential member of a Jewish family, Alphonse Ratisbonne. A convert friend tried to reason with him, but Ratisbonne was adamant. At the height of the discussion, his friend, who had great faith in the Miraculous

Medal, gave him one and asked him to wear it. Amused, Ratisbonne promised to do so. He even allowed his friend's daughter to tie the medal around his neck. He also agreed to recite the *Memorare*. A few days later, as he waited for a friend in a church in Rome, his attention was drawn to a great burst of illumination coming from one of the chapels. So great was it that he felt blinded. He stood blinking, unable to bear the light.

Impelled to look, he walked over in the direction of the strange brilliance. Suddenly he stopped, frightened. There, with her hands stretched out lovingly, as if waiting to embrace the whole world, was our Lady, just as she had appeared to Catherine in the chapel at the rue du Bac. She made a sign to him to kneel. He fell before her. When he lifted his eyes, the light was unbearable. He could raise them only as far as the hands of our Lady. Instantly he was converted. When his friend returned, Ratisbonne told him of his experience. "I understood all", he said.

Not long afterward, Alphonse Ratisbonne became a Catholic. Soon after his baptism, he decided to study for the priesthood. He consecrated his life to the conversion of his brother Israelites in the Congregation of Our Lady of Sion. This experience of such an internationally known man drew great attention to the Miraculous Medal and its power.

Ratisbonne was one of the many people who wished to speak to the Sister who had been the means of giving the medal to the world. He wrote to the rue du Bac asking for the privilege. But Father Aladel answered every such request with the same reply: "The Sister who received the visions of our Lady desires to remain unknown."

The Pope himself wore a Miraculous Medal. His Holiness also wished to know the religious who had been honored by the Blessed Virgin. But humble Catherine remained silent, as the Queen of Heaven had desired, and wished only to be known as the Sister of the poultry yard. It did not matter that some of her companions thought this the right kind of work for her. Catherine was always the first to agree that, since she could not read or write well, she was quite suited to take care of the chickens. All that mattered was that she do her work as well as possible.

News of the medal was avidly sought after. The Miraculous Medal magazine was in enormous demand. As fast as the presses rolled, the magazine spread like wildfire. Father Aladel himself had written a book on the subject of the medal and its wonders. Four complete editions were sold before the end of the first year.

Monsieur Vachette, busier than he had ever been in his life, made a fortune producing the medal, and no fewer than fifteen other firms were at work turning them out. As Father Aladel had said, "You will find yourself a rich man, in more ways than one." The old engraver often thought of those words.

Sometimes, while Catherine was sweeping or working in the garden, the thought of our Lady's statue troubled her. When would Father Aladel stop hesitating? Did he not yet believe that Mary wanted it as much as she did the medal? Time passed, and although she seized every opportunity to ask Monsieur Aladel about Our Lady of the Globe, nothing was done. Catherine suffered over these delays, but she always kept her troubles to herself.

In the year 1841, the tables were turned. It was Father Aladel who came to Sister Catherine with a request. "There is something I want you to do, *ma soeur*", he said. "Please write out a complete account of the apparitions. Leave nothing out. Express everything you saw and felt."

Catherine whitened to the lips. For a moment she could not utter a word and found herself trembling. Her throat tightened, but at last she managed to speak. "But you, Monsieur, you are the only person who is to know. Our Lady said . . ."

"As your spiritual director I impose this duty on you."

Sister Labouré recoiled. "But my writing, Monsieur . . . it's . . ."

"I understand that", the priest said, nodding. "But the writing doesn't matter."

"But my spelling . . ."

"Our Lady is no respecter of spelling", replied Father Aladel.

Then the seer of the Queen of Heaven remembered obedience. "Very well", Catherine said quietly.

That very day Sister Labouré began the task to which she had been assigned.

9

THE SECRET OF A SAINT

THE YEARS BROUGHT a measure of peace and contentment to Catherine, but moments of sorrow as well. There had always been a strong suspicion among the community that Sister Labouré was the seer of the Blessed Virgin. From time to time, Catherine was embarrassed by thoughtless remarks and curious questions. And, at the same time, there was deep resentment on the part of some. But why? Catherine always wondered. Of all the Sisters working with her, was she not the simplest? Had not our Lady chosen the least worthy? Why did they seem to treat her with such a mixture of resentment and curiosity?

One person alone had been immediately aware of Sister Labouré's sanctity. That was Sister Séjole. Long ago, when she first welcomed her to Châtillon, she had seen the depth of the young postulant's soul. Never once was she known to murmur under any discomfort, always eager to do the things commanded of her.

When the news reached Châtillon that the Blessed Virgin had appeared to a young novice making her novitiate in Paris, it was Sister Séjole who declared at once, "It must be to Catherine Labouré that she appeared." There was no question in her mind.

Catherine was to find Sister Séjole her dearest friend all through her life. When she visited the orphans at the Reuilly house, Sister Séjole always made a point of walking through the yard and across the gardens to speak to Catherine. They loved to talk over the early days at Châtillon and reminisce about the old people they used to visit together.

Sister Séjole was growing old, and when she returned to Châtillon after her last visit to Enghien, she told her community:

"Listen to me, our Sisters one day will speak of Sister Labouré as the one who had the privilege of seeing our Lady. I shall be dead by then. But I feel certain that those wonderful blue eyes have looked on the Queen of Heaven."

"What makes you think so, Sister?" asked one of the young postulants who had heard the remark.

"I saw a ray of supernatural joy illuminating her face while she spoke of our Blessed Mother. It was unmistakable."

Catherine continued to work along in her quiet way. One fall day she and another Sister were walking in the orchard of the hospice. Catherine had a basket on her arm, and she was going to gather apples. They were laughing about something one of the old pensioners had said the day before, when Catherine's companion became suddenly serious.

"Will you tell me something, *ma soeur*?" she asked.

"Gladly, if you think I know the answer."

Her companion's face was troubled. "I'm not sure if I should ask such a personal question . . . but it's this. How do you make your meditations?"

"Oh," Catherine replied, "it is not difficult. When I go to the chapel, I place myself before the good God, and I say to him: 'Lord, here I am. Give me what you will.' If he gives me nothing, I thank him also, because I do not deserve anything. And then again, I tell him all that passes through my mind. I recount my pains and all my joys . . . and . . . I listen."

In a few simple words Catherine had revealed the secret of saints.

How often the orchard reminded Catherine of her Burgundy home, of dear Tonine and the others. Marie-Louise had wisely and gratefully returned to her convent, and for this Catherine was everlastingly thankful.

Two years before, Tonine's family had moved to Paris. Her daughter Marie was now a young lady. Her son Philippe showed signs of being very clever in school. Claude had found a comfortable little house for the family in the Boulevard Pereire.

Her family was close to Catherine in her prayers, and now she could greet them often in person. That Claude and Tonine should come to live so close to Enghien was like a second springtime in Catherine's life.

Soon after the end of young Philippe's first college term, Tonine proudly brought her son to see Catherine. What a joyous reunion! Looking in astonishment at her nephew, Catherine cried, "Why, he is a young man. I somehow didn't realize. . . . Well, he must be nearly seventeen!"

"Yes", said Tonine, slipping her arm through his. "He is already grown up." Motherly pride radiated from her.

"When I brought you to the Vincentian Fathers in Pans," said his aunt, "I was afraid you'd be a little frightened. I thought of you as just a schoolboy."

Philippe laughed. "I've survived very well, Aunt Zoé. That was all of two years ago!"

"Tell me, how is the Latin coming along?" This was an important matter to Catherine. She hoped he might one day want to be a priest. "I remember that the curé at Vizerny thought you were beginning to show promise.

Tonine opened her handbag and drew out a piece of paper. "Here is the answer, Zoé", she said, handing it over with maternal happiness. It was a report on Philippe's progress from college. He had come out at the top of his class in Latin.

"Don't look so proud", Philippe said to his mother, teasing. "You must admit I would never have gone to college but for Aunt Zoé. Now, would I?"

"As if we could ever forget!"

Catherine's vow of poverty allowed her to accept money sent her by her family for Christmas, Easter, or a feast day. With these offerings she had helped to pay for her nephew's education.

As Catherine looked into the heart of this loved nephew, she saw there courage and faith, the raw materials of sanctity. Then she made one of those prophetic statements which are later remembered and wondered at. Quietly, almost casually, she said, "Our priests will receive you if you wish to enter the Community of Saint Vincent." After a moment's reflection she added, "Philippe, you have not seen our chapel at the Reuilly house. It's just there, through the gardens and across the playground. See the spire above the trees?"

When Philippe left them, Catherine looked into

Tonine's eyes and read something there. "You have a worry running around in your heart, haven't you, Tonine?"

Tonine gratefully confided in her older sister, "It's Claude, Zoé. I'm so concerned and frightened. He has fallen away from the Church . . . and . . ." She was almost in tears.

"I will pray for him. I'll come and talk to him the first moment I'm free", Catherine promised.

But some days later, before Catherine could keep her promise to visit Claude, a message arrived. Marie's scrawl was on the envelope. Tonine had never learned to write. Catherine opened the note: "Please come. Papa is very sick. Mother needs you."

Permission granted, Catherine set off. When she reached the Meugniots' house, Tonine opened the door, her face tear-stained. "Oh! Thank God you have come. Claude is worse. The doctor says he's dying. He won't see a priest." Breathlessly she added: "If anyone can bring him back to God, it's you, Zoé."

"Let me talk to him, Tonine."

"He's being very difficult", Tonine warned, forgetting the cantankerous old men Catherine was so used to managing. When they reached Claude's room, Tonine said: "Zoé's come to see you.

The invalid, propped up on two pillows, looked as fearsome as a hungry lion. He was grumbling at Marie, who hovered around trying to be useful. She succeeded only in knocking a cup to the floor.

"Leave it alone!" he cried, lifting himself up with sudden strength. "You and your mother are forever fussing."

Catherine laid a hand on Tonine's shoulder as if to say be patient, forgive him. She walked over and sat down beside his bed, as Tonine and her daughter left them alone.

The ravages of a long illness had completely changed the face of her brother-in-law. Catherine placed one of her medals into the palm of his hand and closed the fingers over it. Claude Meugniot smiled. Catherine, watching him, remembered his just pride when he spoke once of the possibility of Philippe's becoming a priest. She knew there was much good in him.

"Zoé," he said, "you've tried before to convert me. I've always joked about it, haven't I? But now . . ." His breath caught in his throat.

"Now . . . yes, Claude?"

"Now I do believe in the eternal mercy . . . and I ask forgiveness. Do you think . . . Sister Catherine . . ." It was the first time he had called her by her name in religion. Now it seemed to give him comfort.

She smiled understandingly. The invalid was gathering strength and with it fresh hope. "You wish to receive the sacraments, Claude?"

He nodded his head slowly.

"Then Marie will go for the priest." Catherine rose and left the room closing the door behind her.

"Tonine," she said, "Claude wishes to receive the sacraments."

Tonine's face showed her satisfaction. "Go at once, Marie, for the priest." The next moment the girl stood, bonnet on, ready to leave. Tonine dried her eyes, and a faint smile hovered on her face as she kissed Catherine good-bye.

Not even conscious of the bitter wind that caught at the folds of her cornette as she left Tonine's house, Catherine heard only the words of the medal singing in her heart, "O Mary conceived without sin, pray for us who have recourse to thee."

Claude did not die. Remaining sincere in his faith, he grew better and lived to see yet another winter frosting the windowpanes and great swirls of snow blanketing the city of Paris.

There was soon to be a small celebration among the Sisters at the Reuilly house, to honor Catherine's twenty-fifth year in religion. A quarter of a century since Catherine had made her first vows! Was it possible? Yes, she remembered the date well. May, our Lady's own month, in the year 1835.

She thought back over the years as she sat now, mending linen, her gaze fixed upon the world beyond the playground and the trees. She recalled the moment of her father's refusal. How hard it had seemed then to look up bravely while the voice within kept calling her.

And there had been that other battle, Father Aladel's opposition. How the conflict had torn her soul! But no bitterness against him ever sprang up within—only grief that she had not been able to carry out our Lady's wishes for such a very long time.

Those days of anxiety over the medal were past. She no longer felt those ups and downs of spirit that had beset her during the first years. All she knew now was the quiet after the storm. She smiled to herself as her thoughts drifted happily.

Even the arrival of Sister Dufès, the new superior who seemed destined to try Catherine's patience in a special way, could not disturb her calm spirit. Catherine bowed to every humiliating demand of Sister Dufès, who thought nothing of criticizing her for the most insignificant offenses, even in the presence of others. Years later, when preliminary hearings were being held prior to Catherine's canonization, a Sister testified:

"I felt bound to tell Sister Dufès my astonishment at seeing her scold a venerable Sister so vehemently for the smallest things. 'Let me be', she replied. 'I feel compelled to do it.'"

Being human, Catherine did not find the proud ways of the new superior pleasant. But being also a saint, she took them as a mortification. Catherine's life at Enghien became a battleground. Knowing this, she put into practice her own advice. When one of the novices murmured against those placed over them, she would say: "Remember, little ones, our superiors in the convent represent God."

One young Sister whom she knew had come from a wealthy home complained of her hands. "They are coarsened from scrubbing floors. I've never been used to . . ."

Sister Labouré looked out from under her cornette. "Our dear Saint Vincent de Paul did not *share* his goods with the poor. He gave all he had. So, child, must we." She went on with a twinkle in her eye. "The first year is always the hardest. Persevere."

The novice warmed toward her. "How understanding you are", she exclaimed. "I don't really know why I complained so." She went away smiling.

In the year 1865, Catherine suffered the loss of her director and confessor, Father Aladel. Now she was beset by a nagging fear. What would become of the secret? Who would keep the account she had written about the visions?

Grief welled in her heart. Never again could she speak to him. The struggle of wills that had caused pain to both of them seemed now almost like a dream. She felt close to him through spiritual ties. They were both servants of Mary. His name would be remembered forever in the archives of the rue du Bac: Father Jean-Marie Aladel, director of the Daughters of Charity in Paris who had caused the Miraculous Medal to be struck, Vincentian, apostle of the poor, and friend. . . .

A happy thought suddenly occurred to her. Monsieur Aladel had died on the thirty-fifth anniversary of the first vision of our Lady at the rue du Bac. She found this a spiritual consolation.

One great joy was to recompense Catherine at the solemn funeral of her director. It was the presence of Philippe. He had come not as Sister Labouré's nephew but as Father Meugniot of the Vincentians.

As Catherine stood in the front row of the mourners, beside her superior, she looked across at Philippe, remembering his ordination not so long before. What a magnificent ceremony it had been! And what a joy to know that she had helped! Seeing the glow of pride on his mother's face when he celebrated his first solemn Mass had caused tears to flow down Catherine's cheeks unchecked, tears of happiness. She felt sure that Claude was looking down from heaven upon his son's holy day.

Philippe had the office of thurifer at the burial of Father Aladel. Long afterward he spoke of the radiance that lighted the face of Sister Catherine as her confessor was laid to rest. When he learned of the saintliness of his aunt, years later, he knew that her happiness sprang from recalling the fulfillment of the Miraculous Medal through him, the establishment of the Children of Mary, and the part he had taken in the special wishes the Blessed Virgin had made to her.

When she knelt before the statue of our Lady in the chapel at Reuilly, one special thought gave Catherine joy. Monsieur Aladel was now seeing the beauty of Mary's smile.

He who had been her servant on earth would now be greatly rewarded by her in heaven.

But now, once again, Catherine began to worry about the altar and the statue of Our Lady of the Globe. She must soon ask her new director, Monsieur Chinchon, to follow our Lady's instructions and arrange for the altar.

"I must ask him to begin arrangements for the statue", she told herself. "He will understand. Besides, Monsieur Aladel was his great friend. But I must bide my time. Perhaps it is a little early to ask." She gave a little unhappy sigh. "After so many years of waiting, what is another short time?"

One day Catherine was unexpectedly summoned to the motherhouse. *Eh bien*, she thought, a reprimand now and again won't hurt any of us. But as the horse-drawn bus rattled in the direction of the rue du Bac, she examined her conscience. Did I . . . ? Could I have . . . ? But she could find nothing. Once again the old fear returned, the one that had caused her anxiety when the assignments were being given out. Suppose she were sent far away somewhere? Oh, not that!

The mother general received her kindly. "I thought you would be happy to know", she began, "that you are being considered for the post of superior."

Catherine's heart gave such a leap of fear that she

could not get her breath. There was no gasp of happiness. She looked steadily at the crucifix that hung on the wall behind the mother general and shook her head. "I couldn't. No, I could never undertake anything like that." Her very nature rebelled. "No, *ma mère*. I am sorry.

"*Ma soeur*, you realize that this is an honor", insisted the superior.

"Oh, yes", Catherine replied gravely. "But I am not capable of such a position. Forgive me, most honored Mother, but I seek no glory." She went on with great emotion. "The poultry yard, the old pensioners. . . ." Becoming tongue-tied and trembling, she stopped altogether.

"Very well, *ma soeur*", said Mother General, too wise to press a point. "I shall respect your wishes. This is not a matter of obedience, as you know. You are free to accept or refuse. I shall not pursue the subject further. Just return to your regular duties at Enghien."

How relieved Catherine was! A position of authority was the last thing she wanted in the autumn of her life. Besides, there were so many others who were better educated, young, and enthusiastic. She was not born to rule. To be hidden was what she wanted, concealed like the lilies of the valley that grew in the mossy woods of Fain-les-Moutiers.

"Thank you", said Catherine, slowly getting up from her chair. She was about to lower herself upon her rheumatic knees for a blessing, but the mother superior quickly excused her from kneeling. Catherine had not realized how old she had grown.

When she returned to the Reuilly house that afternoon, she felt like a traveler returning to the home she loved. How dear the big yellow orphanage was, with its many windows and its playground. And the children's voices! She could not bear to think she might never have heard them again.

Then there were the two carved, white figures that decorated the entrance to the chapel, so familiar to her that they seemed almost real. Oh, it was good to be home again!

In the garden was her beloved statue of Mary. As was her custom, she stood before it and offered a short prayer:

"Dear Blessed Mother, thank you for letting me stay here, where I am so happy."

WHITE DOVE, SILVER TRUMPET

I N 1871 PARIS was embroiled once again in a cruel
struggle. The Franco-Prussian War the year before
had resulted in a French defeat, and now a *communard*
uprising sought to put down the weak Third French
Republic. Frenchmen were killing Frenchmen. This
was civil war.

The orphanage and convent at Reuilly were turned
into a hospital. Food became ever scarcer until hunger

made people eat dogs, cats, and even rats. Again barricades were set up in the streets, and armed bands began to force their way into religious houses.

"God have mercy on us!" cried one of the Sisters, when she heard a burst of gunfire in the street. "They will arrest all the priests as they did before."

"Pray!" It was the strong voice of the superior. "Until either of our houses is attacked, we shall go on just as if nothing had happened. We have plenty to do. There is no time for fear."

So far the hospice had been unaffected by the troops of men sent to search convents, but eventually two terror-stricken men appeared at the back door of the Reuilly house. They wore the red and blue uniforms of those who had remained loyal to the government.

"For the love of God, hide us", they begged. They explained that they had become separated from their companions and that the insurgents were after them.

"We shall be shot on sight!" they gasped. "They're out for our blood."

Someone had seen the men enter the orphanage. Next day, just as the Sisters were leaving the chapel, there was a battering on the front door. The butt of a pistol smashed in a panel.

"Open up! Open up!" cried several voices. Although Sister Dufès blocked the path of the rebels, there had not been enough time for the two fugitives to escape from the convent. They were taken prisoner. But Sister Dufès was determined. Knowing that the prisoners would be shot, she bravely followed the captors to plead their cause. "If you leave these two prisoners in my custody, I will be responsible for them", she promised.

She stood before the *communards* like a strong tree, refusing to be swayed. Something in her compelling manner convinced the leader, and he released the prisoners.

On Easter Sunday the *communards* were back at Reuilly. They had changed their minds.

"We've come for the two prisoners", they demanded. "Hand them over!"

When Sister Dufès refused, the furious mob swirled around the entrance to the convent, threatening with fists and curses. The leader lifted his hand for silence, and in that moment one of the Sisters recognized a man whom she herself had fed and nursed.

"How can you be so ungrateful," she asked, "you who came to us begging for help?"

Criticism of one of their own men added fuel to the fire of the mob's anger. They forced their way into the convent in a renewed search for the two gendarmes, but Sister Dufès' tactics had given the hunted men time to hide. One of them discovered an empty bed in the old men's dormitory. He jumped in, pulling the sheets up around his ears. The searchers passed him by without so much as a glance.

Just before the arrival of the *communards*, Father Chinchon, confessor to the Sisters, had visited the convent in the company of a young subdeacon. Father Chinchon had managed to return to the mother-house in time, but the young cleric was still in the convent.

"Couldn't we disguise him?" suggested one of the worried Sisters.

The superior nodded. "An excellent idea, *ma soeur*. But how shall we go about it?"

"In the clothing room", suggested a young Sister, "there are some trousers and blue shirts."

"Yes, and a cap. We must hide his clerical tonsure. Hurry, then, Sisters!"

A few minutes later, dressed as a workman, carrying a loaf of bread under his arm, the subdeacon escaped.

Since the rebels had already threatened to arrest Sister Dufès, the Sisters kept urging their superior to flee to Versailles until the danger passed. Reluctantly she did so, and during this period Catherine proved to be a tower of strength. She carried out the work of the house and directed the charities, which continued as before. When the *communards* occupied part of the convent building, Catherine kept repeating in her heart the words of the Blessed Virgin, "The moment will come when the danger is great. But do not fear. Have confidence. I will protect this house."

Even when she was taken to the *communard* headquarters, Catherine was fearless, knowing that our Lady's promises would be kept. For all their questions she had straightforward answers. It was obvious to the questioners that it had been a mistake to bring such a gentle old Sister before them, and the chief examiner finally ordered, "Escort this Sister back to the hospice, and don't ever bring any of them here again."

On May 18, mobs broke into one of the beautiful churches in Paris and destroyed everything that could be broken. For three days the rioting lasted. Then the Republican troops broke through, and the men of the Commune were routed. Forced to surrender, they gave up their food and munitions. The horrors of the civil war were over, but never would it be forgotten. In Paris alone, six thousand had been slain.

Knowing that those they had held as hostages would be freed, the rebels had their final revenge. They rushed into the dungeons where they had imprisoned the priests and monks, including the archbishop of Paris, Monseigneur Darboy.

At eight o'clock that night the hostages were taken out of their cells and lined up. "Come out and save yourselves. Move fast", shouted their captors. "One at a time." As they emerged into the street they were shot to death.

The saintly archbishop had raised his right arm to give his blessing to those about to die.

"You've given your benediction", voiced the captain of the firing party. "Now take mine."

A bullet entered the archbishop's heart and killed him.

Next morning, when the news reached Father

Chinchon, the Sisters' confessor, he remembered the prophecy made to Sister Labouré in 1830: the archbishop would be martyred in forty years' time.

Catherine had always loved the ceremonies in the month of Mary. Many times in her childhood she had taken part in the fêtes that abounded in the villages of Burgundy. Finally forced to leave the Reuilly house for safety's sake, she had taken along with her the narrow gilt coronet belonging to the statue of Mary in the chapel, promising that on the day the Sisters returned safely she would re-crown her. On May 31, Catherine fulfilled that promise. Her heart was brimming over with love as she made a little ceremony of replacing the gilt circlet.

"Hail, Queen of Angels," she whispered, "we have returned home, grateful and happy." Then slowly, painfully, she got down on her knees and bowed her head.

The face of Catherine Labouré did not change much in the evening of her life. Age brought with it a new wisdom. She watched over her old men as long as her rheumatism and asthma allowed.

Every morning she walked through the long garden between the two houses to the chapel, in snow and in rain. Often she was there before the others.

When a kind Sister offered Catherine a cushion for her knees during the long hours of prayer, she replied that the discomfort reminded her of the happiness she had experienced in the Labouré chapel in Fain as a child. "Those old flagstones were colder than any here", she said with a smile.

But while she dwelt on earth, Catherine's mind and soul were fixed on heaven. She thought God had asked so little of her in her old age—to give up the duties she loved and contentedly watch someone else perform them. She made a point of encouraging new Sisters starting out on their first missions, promising to pray for them, admonishing gently when they complained.

Once, as Catherine was walking in the garden at Enghien with young Sister Cosnard, she said quietly, "One day we shall leave this place."

For a moment her young companion looked at her with a startled expression. "But, *ma soeur*, how do you know?"

"I see it", Catherine replied. "I see the place where my dear old pensioners will live. It is very beautiful— a castle, in fact. Near it is a river. I see over the doorway the words 'Hospice d'Enghien' written in gold."

Sister Cosnard was a little frightened. She had heard vague rumors that Catherine might be the Sister of the visions. But no one knew for certain.

A glorious smile made Catherine's face shine. "I can see the old men. They're very happy . . . and they're wearing uniforms of dark blue."

Twenty years after Catherine's death, all this came about as she had predicted.

The years passed gently, like shadows. Catherine had a strong presentiment that she would not live to see the end of another year. She spoke of her death, but her listeners only shrugged off her words. A Sister is always preparing for death, they thought. But Catherine knew better.

Suddenly she was appalled when she realized what she had *not* done. The statue and the altar had not yet been made. What would our Lady say to her? Soon she would be called to account. The statue must be started before she said good-bye to this world.

"I've failed in my mission", she kept telling herself. "There's so little time left."

Then came a decisive blow. Father Chinchon, the only person who knew her story, was suddenly removed from his post as confessor to the Sisters. For ten years, poor Catherine had been urging him to have the statue made. Now she became so distraught that she took upon herself an unheard-of mission. She would go to the superior general of the Vincentian Fathers and ask him to let Father Chinchon continue as her confessor.

Bravely she armed herself, like a knight going to do battle, determined to take her stand in our Lady's cause. She managed to gain admittance, and the kind superior listened to her plea to have her confessor restored. But he knew nothing of Sister Labouré. He looked upon her petition as the caprice of an aged person.

"I'm sorry, *ma soeur*, but I see no reason to accord such a favor. I'm sorry to disappoint you", he said. He had no way of knowing that the courageous woman before him was the Sister of the visions.

Catherine returned from her unsuccessful mission shaken and tearful. To Sister Dufès' kind inquiry, she replied that she had something to tell her but she would have to ask our Lady first. The following morning, having spoken to our Lady in her prayers and having received a favorable reply, Catherine proceeded to tell her superior the full story of the visions and the still-unfulfilled request for the statue.

Sister Dufès listened with amazement and with unaccustomed sympathy. Then she assured Catherine decisively, "The statue and the altar shall be designed according to your description. I must obtain proper permission, of course, but do not worry about that. Set your mind at rest, *ma soeur*."

Weeks went by before the drawings were approved by the superiors. But at last the statue of the Virgin with the Globe was finished. When Sister Dufès took Sister Labouré to see it in the sculptor's studio, Catherine exclaimed, disappointedly, "Oh, the Blessed Virgin was so much more beautiful than that!" But she could rest happily now. The torment was over. At last she had accomplished our Lady's wishes. The new altar

was in hand already, and all her secrets had been dis-
closed.

Commonplace as her labors had been, Catherine
Labouré had done them with all her heart. In her shy,
modest way she had accomplished great things. Now,
in her seventieth year, her heart and will were united
to God as they had been since the age of nine.

Sometimes, at night when she lay awake, the years
rolled back. She fancied she heard the voices of Papa
and the other children getting ready for the trip to
Senailly.

"Who wants to sit on the driver's seat with me?"

"Oh, imagine asking that!" cried Mama. "You know
they all want to sit up there with you!" How pretty
Mama looked!

There was Tonine with her doll, and eleven-year-
old Joseph, busy polishing the shoes before Mama
packed them. And Ninette, the cat. Whatever had become of her?

Smiling inwardly, she fancied she could hear the
pigeons circling round excitedly, alighting on her
shoulder, pecking at each other jealously as she came
into the yard, her apron full of golden grain. A church
bell chimed across the night, breaking into her reverie.
She wasn't sure whether it floated out from their own
chapel at Reuilly or from the pointed belfry of the
church at Moutiers-Saint-Jean. It didn't matter. Such a
lovely, peaceful sound! "You were born, Catherine,

just as the evening Angelus was ringing", Papa had told her. Perhaps that was why she loved the chiming of bells.

Her thoughts turned to the statue of Our Lady of the Globe. "It is a poor thing, Blessed Mother," she whispered, "but what earthly creature could fashion your beauty?"

Just as she was falling into a light sleep, she whispered to our Lady, "The altar will soon be there, in the place where you stood, with the golden ball in your hands."

In her hand she clasped a medal, one of the first, given her by Father Aladel. Yesterday Catherine had made several small packages of them, to be given to those she loved best. But the one in her hand was for Tonine's grandchild. Marie's little one would soon be making her First Communion. . . . Such a beautiful child, God bless her.

Dozing off, Catherine thought of each member of her family, praying for them, keeping every one of them in a secret room in her heart, that they might fulfill the mission in life that God had entrusted to them. "O Mary conceived without sin, pray for us who have recourse to thee."

On the last day of the year, Sister Catherine Labouré died. With her death her glory began. The first cure obtained through her intercession took place a few days after her death. In due time her reputation for sanctity spread. In 1907 the Cause of Sister Catherine was introduced at Rome, and on December 11 of that year she received the title "Venerable". In May 1933, she was beatified.

Fourteen years later, before a great assemblage of cardinals, bishops, and thousands of people, the voice of His Holiness Pope Pius XII solemnly declared Catherine Labouré a saint.

Joining in with the princes of the Church, the voices of those present rose in a mighty *Te Deum* of praise. The great bells of the basilica sent out a swelling paean of triumph. The gentle Sister whose life had been one of humble mortification was proclaimed a member of the Church Triumphant.

Beside the cardinals stood fifteen bishops wearing white miters. Patriarchs from the Orient stood with members of the diplomatic corps. Along with other offerings presented to His Holiness were three gilt cages containing white birds and turtledoves. When the silver trumpets heralded the new saint, the birds were released, symbolizing purity and peace.

In contrast with her life of submissive obedience, henceforth Saint Catherine Labouré would have her own feast day in the calendar of God's beloved servants. The Blessed Virgin herself had sought Catherine out that she should be brought triumphantly from her hiding place.

AUTHOR'S NOTE

I am indebted to Farrar, Straus, and Cudahy for the privilege of reading in manuscript form the excellent biography *Saint Catherine Labouré of the Miraculous Medal*, by Joseph I. Dirvin, C.M.

Other books that I have found helpful are *La Vie secrète de Catherine Labouré*, by Antoinette Huzzard; *The Silence of Saint Catherine*, by Madame Louis-Lefebvre; and *A History of the Paris Commune of 1871*, by G. B. Benham.

While the major incidents of Saint Catherine's life here described are based on historical fact, I have reconstructed the settings and invented dialogue to bring the scenes to life.

Personal thanks are due to the Reverend Joseph A. Skelly, C.M., Director of the Central Association of the Miraculous Medal, Germantown, Pennsylvania, who so generously gave of his time when I visited there to see the Miraculous Medal Museum. In this treasure house I was privileged to see, among other things, much of the regalia used in the canonization of Saint Catherine in Rome.

Grateful thanks are due also to the Sisters of Charity at Emmitsburg, Maryland, who kindly supplied much material. I am also deeply indebted to Sister Marie Dubuisson of the Daughters of Charity, No. 140 rue du Bac, for taking me through parts of the convent so closely associated with Saint Catherine Labouré. I also wish to thank the Sister at No. 77 rue de Reuilly who showed me the chapel at the Reuilly house, where the heart of Saint Catherine reposes in a crystal reliquary. Under this chapel is a vault where Saint Catherine's bed and her missal are preserved.

A. P.–W.